Using her past experience as a clergy wife and a state school librarian, Claire Gathercole's writing explores how she and others can cope with the problems life throws at us, often when we least expect them. From the grief encountered at different times by everyone, she explores ways to find the love and hope we all need to survive as we look to the future.

This story is dedicated to the real 'Hetty' – not her actual name – whose survival from the wartime dilemma she encountered inspired me to write this novel.

Claire Gathercole

HETTY

Welcome to Ombersley, Louise!

Claire Gathercole

AUSTIN MACAULEY PUBLISHERS™

LONDON · CAMBRIDGE · NEW YORK · SHARJAH

A CIP catalogue record for this title is available from the British Library.

ISBN 9781528991988 (Paperback)
ISBN 9781528991995 (ePub e-book)

www.austinmacauley.com

First Published (2020)
Austin Macauley Publishers Ltd
25 Canada Square
Canary Wharf
London
E14 5LQ

I am indebted to many folks who helped me in the writing of this book. Firstly, a creative writing degree course at Birmingham University when I first wrote this novel. Then more recently to the novel-writing course at Marlborough Summer School in 2018. However, it is local friends and family who have encouraged me to get it published. In particular, I must mention my good friends Sue Johnson, Iris Checketts and Marie Smart, who read and made many helpful suggestions, not forgetting my granddaughter, Ella Waters, who was able to give a younger reader's advice. Other family and friends, including Sue Smith and Pat King, have also helped me greatly as I thought about how to get my novel published and promoted to as wide a public as possible.

1945

The telegram had said:

Second Lieutenant Will Thomas will be repatriated on Monday 12th March and should arrive home two days later.

Hetty had bought yards of red, white and blue bunting to decorate. Mary's small hands were enthusiastic rather than helpful. *Welcome Home Will* was written large on the outside of the house.

Mary was beside herself with excitement and Hetty with apprehension.

The wireless was playing as she scrubbed the floor, grubby from baking cakes and pies for his return, with her face glowing pink from the exercise.

She didn't hear Will quietly open the back door and jumped out of her skin when he spoke.

"That's a fine way to greet your husband, scrubbing! I expected you in your best bib and tucker, waiting for me with Mary sitting on your knee."

Hetty let out a shriek, "Will, I can't believe it! You weren't due for two days yet." She whipped off her apron and untied her hair.

"I would have been sitting waiting if you'd warned me exactly when you were coming."

She realised she was talking just for the sake of it, to cover up her shock. "I was trying to get everything perfect for our reunion."

"I got a lift to London on an army vehicle and made record time." He grinned.

Neither of them moved. They just stood and stared at each other. *He had changed,* thought Hetty. He looked haggard and thin and his face had a closed-in and guarded look. He must have suffered. It was written all over his face.

Her heart went out to him and she moved towards him.

"Well, haven't you got a kiss for your husband then? Aren't you pleased to see me? I haven't changed so much you don't recognise me, have I?"

"Of course, you haven't." Hetty lifted her face to his, but she knew she was lying. His kiss, when it came, was demanding and gave her no time to draw breath.

"Wow," a gasp as he finally released her. "You don't waste time, do you!"

"I'm making up for all the time I've lost. Where's Mary, by the way?"

"She's at school," said Hetty. "I go to fetch her at 3.30."

"Good, I'll come with you and before that, we've got time to go upstairs for a bit."

"Hang on!" Hetty could feel herself panicking. How could she go upstairs and make love when Will now felt like a complete stranger?

"Wouldn't you like a cup of tea first? And I've made a lovely cake! Anyway, surely you'd like me to tidy myself up and put on some nice clothes!"

"I'll come and help you tidy yourself up if you like, although you look pretty good as you are. But there are more important things than a cup of tea and a slice of cake. We can have those later when Mary gets home."

But what Hetty discovered in the bedroom helped her to overcome her panic and give herself to Will in a way she had not thought possible.

She bit her lip when she saw how visible his rib cage was and how scraggy his body looked. He had been a beautiful young man with a well-covered body. But worse was to come. As he stripped off his shirt, Hetty let out a gasp.

"Don't look, please don't look." He turned to face her so that she couldn't see his back, but it was too late as she had already caught a glimpse. It was criss-crossed with great weals. Will had been badly tortured.

Realising all that he had been through, how on earth was she going to be able to tell him about baby Dorothy?

Part One
1942

The doorbell rang.

She ran to answer it, the toddler dragging at her skirt.

Her heart leapt in her mouth when she saw the post boy and his bike and yellow telegram.

It simply said, *MISSING, PRESUMED DEAD.*

She felt like lead.

---ooo000ooo---

It was twelve months later, in September 1943, that Hetty was persuaded to get away and take little Mary to stay with her husband's parents in Somerset. The meagre pension she now received, as Will was presumed dead, was barely enough to feed and clothe them both but her parents paid for her fare and the child still travelled free. *It would get the mother and child away from the bombing,* they thought. Hetty, their younger daughter, was especially precious to them.

She was a fine sight, slender and straight with white blond hair which she tied up with rags at night to curl the ends. Her clothes were hand-me-downs, as were little Mary's, but she carried herself well and the heavy wool coat swung as she walked, while the bright scarf around her neck told of her strength of will to survive.

It was easiest to wear the coat she would need in the winter months to come and fortunately, although it had been a mild spring and a hot dry summer, it was now becoming cooler. In fact, Hetty was keeping an eye on the clouds as it looked rather like rain and she had no brolly to shield them from a downpour.

It was a slow stopping train they took from London but at least she only had to change once at Bristol and people were kind. The young mother and child drew the odd smile and kindly word from older women on the train, while the two young soldiers travelling in the same compartment vied with each other to amuse Mary and get a smile of gratitude from Hetty.

With a final puff of steam and scream of brakes, the train drew into Wells and there, waiting for her on the platform was her husband's mother, Mavis, with a warm smile. She was dressed in a raincoat with a headscarf, Hetty noticed. Perhaps she was worried about rain too.

Mavis had always been welcoming to her daughter-in-law, although her husband, Arnold, was dour and difficult to please.

"Good journey? And how's my little granddaughter then? My, how you've grown!"

Mary just about managed a smile for the grandmother she barely knew as she clung to her mother's coat.

"She'll soon feel at home with us, I'm sure." Mavis smiled.

"It is so good of you to bring her—especially in the circumstances…" her voice broke. "Come on now," she braced herself, "the bus to our village leaves in 10 minutes and we'll have to hurry to catch it."

Hetty smiled sadly. It was going to be difficult to cope with her mother-in-law's grief as well as her own.

What she hadn't reckoned on was the effect that grief had on Arnold. He hardly moved from his armchair and only put his newspaper down while the BBC News was broadcast.

He had never been easy, but now she was lucky to get a word out of him and she had the strong impression that somehow, he blamed her for Will's fate. In his mind, it was Hetty who had taken Will, an only child and the apple of his eye, from his native environment to the big city of London and that was the beginning of the end.

He was a good-looking young man, almost too sure of himself but nevertheless popular with his peers for his sense of humour and liveliness. And he was bright. Wells Grammar

School had been proud of him and he won the Maths Prize in his final year.

Will had married Hetty at the very beginning of the war in October 1939. They had been courting since he arrived in North London and started attending the same Methodist Church as Hetty and her family.

The boy from Somerset had been pleased to overcome his parents' opposition and get himself a job in London, working with a firm of accountants.

The advent of war had been the spur to a serious commitment between many couples who got married in haste, determined not to miss out on this experience at least, amidst all the uncertainty and anxiety. Hetty and Will were no exception and engagement and marriage followed within the hurried space of six weeks, giving them six months of married life before Will was called up. Mary was born in August 1940 and Will got 24 hours compassionate leave to come and see his wife and new baby.

He had managed one more week of leave before the foreign posting came when Mary was nine months old, by which time he was in the Royal Engineers, where his mathematical ability was appreciated.

---ooo000ooo---

The routine of Hetty and Mary's life at 14 Wells Road was soon established. A small, three-bedroomed terrace house, it nevertheless had a long garden like its neighbours. And a long garden was a boon as it enabled them to grow vegetables and keep chickens.

Mary learnt to feed the hens in the morning and loved the job of seeking out the warm eggs later in the day.

Hetty helped Mavis with the shopping and cleaning and offered help with the garden—which was only grudgingly allowed by Arnold.

Mavis was a good manager and a good cook, and meals though basic, were plentiful.

Mary was still at the fussy stage and cried when she was made to eat up the greens that Arnold had grown in the garden, while stealing as many sultanas as Mavis would allow from her kitchen cupboard.

Supplementary food was always available in the nearby fields and hedgerows and along with many other mums and their children, Hetty trawled the lanes and fields for blackberries and rosehips, mushrooms and nuts.

Mary loved these adventures and dropping the glossy berries into her mother's basket—as well as quite a few into her mouth. And for once she didn't have to keep her clothes clean. Old clothes were the order of the day so that a few bramble stains did not matter.

The villagers soon got used to the newcomer in their midst and although slightly wary of her London ways, they knew the tragedy of Will's disappearance and went out of their way to welcome her and the child.

---ooo000ooo---

The blackberries were luscious that year: big, black and shiny, and it was on one such blackberrying outing that she first met David.

He was the local schoolteacher and on a nature trail with the children, collecting berries for their mothers as they went. Tall and dark, he had a faintly abstracted air as if he was always thinking of something else.

One of the children, over-excited and running, bumped into her as he ran ahead, spilling both his berries and hers.

"I'm so sorry," David hurried to her.

"Johnny, you really must look where you are going. Help us pick these up now."

"Sorry, missus," Johnny hung his head.

Hetty laughed.

"It's all right. I expect you'd seen some better ones ahead, had you?"

David looked at her. What a girl! Shining, fair and slender. The local girls were mostly dark and of a plumper build. And they didn't laugh easily. It took a long while to get them beyond the suspicious and slightly surly stage.

"You're not from these parts," he noticed the child, Mary, as he spoke. "What brings you down to this backwater?"

"I'm on a visit to my parents-in-law." She noticed his kind eyes. "They hadn't seen Mary for ages, and I thought it might cheer them up in the circumstances."

"Have they had bad news then?"

"We all have, sadly. My husband was reported 'Missing, presumed dead' a year ago now."

"That must be very hard for you all."

His eyes roamed his flock of children.

"I must take this lot back to their mothers now or my name will be mud if they are late."

"Yes, of course. And we must get on with our picking. Mary, come on, love."

Mary didn't want to disengage herself from the motherly hands of two little schoolgirls who had taken her under their wings.

"But I want to go with them." Mary stamped her small foot.

"Yes, why don't you?" David was reluctant to let them go.

"It looks as if you've got plenty of berries already and I'll top you up with some of mine. It's good for the little one to have company."

So Mary joined David's class of children and he and Hetty chatted casually with each other and the children, while they all made their way back to the village.

"I run a youth club on Tuesday evenings from 7–8.30 if you're ever at a loose end and would like to come and help."

David ventured as they parted at the school gate.

"It's in the Methodist Church Hall. You'd be very welcome."

"Thanks, that's a kind offer. I'll see how the land lies and if my parents-in-law are happy to babysit."

"I've always had lots of youngsters around me in church at home and enjoy their company, so I'd like to help if I can."

19

---ooo000ooo---

It was difficult for Hetty in the evenings. Arnold read the paper and grumbled at the news in it, while Mavis knitted.

Mary was expected to go to bed at six o'clock and not be seen or heard again till the next morning.

She found this difficult to begin with and Hetty spent many an evening sitting quietly in the bedroom with her until she slept. However, she was gradually improving and latterly Hetty had got downstairs within the hour.

This was no great advantage as Arnold didn't hold with women's chatter and she and Mavis were expected to sit quietly while knitting and sewing.

"We met David Holman, the schoolteacher, out in the lane with the children when we were blackberrying the other day," Hetty broke the silence one evening.

"He asked if I would like to help with the youth club on Tuesday evenings. It's held in the Methodist Church Hall."

She knew that Arnold and Mavis were keen churchgoers. Mavis smiled.

"Well, that's really nice. It would do you good to get out a bit and I'm sure you'd be useful at the club. Mrs Davies, down the road, also helps. She'll take you along with her next Tuesday if you ask, I'm sure."

Mrs Davies was a cheery soul, probably in her forties, Hetty thought, when she called for her at 6.45 the next Tuesday. She was good company and enthusiastic both about the youth club and the children who attended, and about David who ran it.

"He is so imaginative in what he does with them and they love him. He really has a gift with them.

"He has to be careful, though. He gets bad asthma, so he can't do anything too strenuous. In one way that's lucky for us, though, as it means he won't be called up into the army even if schoolteachers cease to be a reserved occupation."

David hurried across when he saw Hetty and Mrs Davies arrive.

"I'm so glad you could come. Today it would be useful if you would spend time getting to know the youngsters. If we're not too daunting for you and you'd like to continue coming, we'll find out if there's anything special you'd like to do with them."

Hetty smiled around at some of the young people near her.

"I'm sure I shall enjoy myself."

"But I'm not so sure what I can do with them. I sew a bit of course—I have to in order to clothe Mary."

Hetty's easy manner and quick smile soon had her surrounded by a crowd. The boys, anxious to impress this lovely looking girl, were keen to know about her husband's army career—and then embarrassed when they heard what had happened.

The girls were more interested to hear about Mary.

When she was asked to play table tennis, she knew she had been accepted and the evening soon passed.

"You will come again next week, won't you," one of the older girls called out to her as she was leaving.

"I'd love to. I've enjoyed myself."

David caught her on the way out.

"Thank you so much for coming."

"She's been a real help, hasn't she?" He smiled across at Mrs Davies as he held the door open for them both.

"A definite asset I should say." Mrs Davis was enthusiastic.

"She's young enough to be on the same wavelength as some of those girls and that will be a great help."

"Shall we see you next week? Or have we put you off for ever?"

"Of course, I'll come. Thank you for inviting me."

---ooo000ooo---

Hetty had been going to the youth club for about five weeks when David caught her again on her way out.

"There's *Henry V* coming on at the Cinema next week. Would you like to come?"

"I'd love to." She hadn't been near a cinema since Will left.

"There's an evening performance on Thursday. Shall I meet you outside the cinema, or can I call for you?"

"We'd better meet up at the cinema, I think. Arnold might get the wrong impression if you call for me."

"I'll meet you outside the cinema at 7.00 then. There's bound to be a queue."

Mary was grizzly on Thursday and didn't want to settle down and sleep.

"Don't worry, I'll sit with her." Mavis enjoyed time with her little granddaughter.

"They say it's a wonderful film." She was rather envious knowing that Arnold would never be persuaded to go and as a respectable married woman she couldn't possibly go on her own.

"Go on, now. I shall look forward to hearing all about it."

The Gaumont Pathe News was just starting as they took their seats. Although cheerful as always, Hetty was not impressed as she read behind the encouraging voice of the newsreader to the graver news behind.

Will had been in the Far East—that's where the telegram giving news of him had come from. She caught her breath and shivered as the reader briefly mentioned the ruthlessness of the Japanese.

David put out a hand to her.

"Are you all right?"

"The telegram we had about Will was from the Far East."

"Not knowing what happened or is happening is not easy. I really hadn't imagined him in quite the sort of situation they showed then—but I suppose he could have been. Oh dear, it sounds absolutely brutal."

"I'm sorry." She felt embarrassed as tears sprung to her eyes.

"It's somehow harder to bear down here with so much to remind me of him in his parents' house. And his father is so difficult. He doesn't like me and gives me the impression that he thinks it's all my fault."

"I'd forgotten we'd get the news," David patted her hand.

"You mustn't torment yourself thinking what might have happened. If he's dead, it's over now and he's at peace. That's what you must hold on to."

As the lights went on again briefly before the main film, he glanced across at her, concern in his eyes.

"You loved him very dearly, didn't you?"

Hetty nodded, drying her eyes, and then asked herself the same question as the lights went out again and they sat in the dark briefly, waiting for the film to begin.

Did she love him very dearly?

Of course, she loved him. The whirlwind effect of their brief engagement before they married had been romantic and exciting.

Her friends in the dress shop where she worked had been very envious of her and she was allowed to use the shop's facilities to sew her own wedding dress in the evenings. *They had all enjoyed the vicarious excitement,* she thought, *and that had somehow heightened her own.*

Of course, she loved him, but the honeymoon wasn't an unqualified success.

Like other young people at the time, and especially their contemporaries at the Methodist Church, they had never ventured beyond the kissing stage of courtship. They had not thought it quite right even to read about the physical side of marriage and the thought of contraception had not even entered their heads.

Of course, she loved him, but their love-making that first night was brief and painful.

Will seemed happy and content and fell into a deep sleep immediately afterwards while she lay awake for a long time confused as to what marriage was really about.

Of course, she loved him, but once they were married, Will no longer took her out and held her hand and kissed her.

She had looked forward to spending whole evenings with him with love making as a natural conclusion. What happened was very different.

Of course, she loved him, but he behaved as if he had a licence to intercourse whenever he wanted it.

Her role was to submit, no matter how tired she was, so that she began to understand what the old 'headache' joke was about.

There was no tenderness or fun in any of it.

She suddenly realised that David was watching her face and she blushed, wondering whether he had read her thoughts.

"Not all plain sailing perhaps." He smiled.

"I believe it never is. Here comes the main film. That should cheer us up."

David didn't forget that desolate look he caught a glimpse of. *I hope he was kind to her,* he thought.

But, of course—Will Thomas—he remembered him. They had been at school together. Will was a year older than he was. He always had lots of girls around him but didn't allow himself to get too close to any of them. He was too ambitious to be bothered with them.

Surely, he would have changed and grown up and realised that girls were not just possessions you picked up and put down.

A lovely girl like Hetty should have changed him.

Any man worth his salt would go out of his way to please her—wouldn't he? I certainly would.

The thought slipped into his mind before he could stop it. She was the sort of girl who needed to be loved and he'd like to be the one who did it. She had such spirit.

He hadn't thought of anyone in this way for a long time now. And he'd better stop quickly. She wasn't free. But if only she was...

He held her hand briefly in the darkness as he said goodbye after walking her to the end of the road where she lived.

"Thank you for coming with me," he said. "It wouldn't have been the same on my own."

"I wouldn't have been allowed to go on my own," Hetty laughed.

"Cinemas aren't really approved of—but fortunately Arnold and Mavis thought I was going with a party of young people from the youth club."

"Did they, indeed?" David held her eyes for a moment and smiled and felt happier than he expected as he walked away.

At least there was nothing to prevent him enjoying her company for the time being. There were very few young people their age left in the village and it would surely be quite natural for them to get together a bit.

Hetty too, walked with a lighter step as she ran home.

She told her mother-in-law of the wonderful way Laurence Olivier had played Henry V, and especially of the night-time scenes at the two camps of the French and the English.

"Then there was an incredible mounted charge by the French. The music accompanying it is still ringing in my head."

"I do wish you could go to see it too, Mavis. The 'St Crispin Day' speech was inspirational and somehow managed to make sense of much of the nonsense of war."

"It would take something to do that," Mavis sighed.

---ooo000ooo---

It was only a week later that David came up to her at the youth club with another proposal.

"The girls here are enjoying the sewing you are doing with them and you are obviously good at it. I was wondering…would you, could you possibly help us with some costumes for the school play?"

"I'd love to," Hetty's eyes shone. "It will be good to make something that isn't useful for a change."

She did not add that it was fun doing things with David, but she felt that too. She felt very relaxed with him and yet

25

there was a spark there. He was always challenging her in some way or another.

"What are you doing?"

"The little ones always do a nativity play at Christmas and their mums take care of the simple costumes for that."

"It's the older children who need help. They're putting on an entertainment."

"When their dads were at home before the war, we used to do a pantomime of sorts, with a lot of the local community involved, as well as the children.

"For the time being it's just the children, of course, and imaginative costumes are a great help. I'm sure you could produce something for Boadicea, for instance—but there's Robin Hood as well."

"Each class is doing something different. There are only four teachers and so many children—we've had a lot of evacuees here as you can imagine—so we are pretty desperate for some help."

"Perhaps I'd better come along after school some time." Hetty thought that she and Mary were probably classed as evacuees as well.

"Is that when you rehearse?"

"Yes, we practise the older ones for half an hour after school every day, so any day will do. I take Class 4—the oldest children—so come and find me."

"I'll be along tomorrow. Does it matter if I bring Mary, too?"

"No, of course, not. There'll always be some girls who will enjoy looking after her."

Bright coloured materials—or indeed any material—was not easy to come by during the war, but Hetty soon had her girls at the youth club scouring through their mums and grandmothers' wardrobes for anything they didn't wear.

Granddads did not escape either and even long pants that were holey and had seen better days were carefully mended, dyed and put to good use as 'hose' for some of Robin Hood's merry men.

As 'black-out' was the order of the day at everyone's windows, Hetty asked those who had curtains of bright coloured linens to lend them to be used as cloaks—promising to take the greatest care of them and return them to be re-hung after the performance.

David marvelled at her skill and imagination and also at the rapport she built up with the school children.

He kept a close eye on all she was doing, ostensibly for the sake of the children and the entertainment, but also, he admitted to himself, because he was fascinated by her and the way she managed to give herself to the children in spite of her current impossible situation.

He enjoyed her company and found that he needed at least a daily dose of it.

Needless to say, the entertainment was a great success. The whole village turned out for it, including Mavis and Arnold.

"Well done, love," Mavis was delighted with her work. "You really made the whole thing look professional with your costumes."

Even Arnold grunted his appreciation. *High praise, indeed,* thought Hetty.

---ooo000ooo---

Having established the routine of visiting the school at the end of the day, Hetty found herself continuing to pop in after it was all over.

She was a welcome guest with the other teachers as well as the children, and David had enlisted her help to teach some of the older girls in his class basic sewing and how to adapt, enlarge and mend old clothing—all very necessary in wartime.

This made her popular with their mums as well, who were always short of clothing coupons and often at their wit's end if their son or daughter was growing quickly and nothing would fit.

But one day when she arrived to teach her group, she found David sitting down at his table, his face as white as a sheet. The children had reading books in front of them but were talking quietly at the same time.

"Are you all right?" Hetty queried. "You look terrible."

She could hear that his breath was laboured and wheezy.

"He gets like this in the winter." One of the older girls in his class liked to be the spokesperson.

"He says it's called asthma," she spoke importantly. "We just have to sit quiet."

"I see." Hetty was dismayed. She turned quietly to David.

"Are you sure you ought to be here? I could stay with the class now if you think that would be all right, and then you could get home early and get to bed."

David was pleased by her concern.

"I suppose you could. But are you sure you don't mind? I get these attacks fairly regularly, but I don't usually feel as bad as this."

"Of course, I don't mind. It's only half an hour till the end of school anyway, and it's not as if the children don't know me."

"Thank you so much."

David would really rather have stayed now that Hetty had arrived but knew that he wouldn't make it home at all if he did.

"I'll tell Mrs Williams that you're here on my way out."

"Good night, children. Mrs Thomas is going to look after you now, while I go home early as I don't feel well. I'm sure you'll look after her nicely, as usual."

He hurried off, stooping slightly, with his breath still coming in awkward gasps.

Hetty quite enjoyed having his class to herself and the time till the home bell flew by.

Mrs Williams put her head in the classroom door as the last few children were leaving.

"Thank you so much, Mrs Thomas. The cold weather always seems to get to David. He has such a weak chest."

"Oh, dear! I suppose it will mean we are without him for several days now. He always tries to struggle in if he possibly can, but the fact that he has given in and gone home must mean that he feels really poorly."

Hetty was concerned.

"How will you manage? It must be very hard for you—and for the children."

"Yes, it is. We shall just have to divide his class up between the other three classes—and that's not good for them or for the children in the other classes."

"I don't mind helping. If I'd be of any use, that is. I'm not a teacher, as you know, but I might be able to help in some way. Mavis would love to look after Mary on her own for a day or two, I'm sure."

"Yes, I suppose you could help," Mrs Williams was thoughtful.

"The children are used to you and respond well to you already. If you could divide your time between the classes, it would be a great help.

"You could do sewing and knitting with them—and some artwork if you like. David said that you painted one of the backdrops for the entertainment... Is that right?"

"Yes, I did, but it was a bit slapdash." Hetty laughed. "We were so short of time towards the end."

"That's settled then," Mrs Williams gave a relieved sigh. "Are you sure you're happy and that you know what you're letting yourself in for?"

"Yes, of course I do. I'll see you in the morning then."

---ooo000ooo---

She had been helping fulltime at the school for four days when Marion Hopes, one of David's class came up to her.

"Do you know how Mr Holman is, Miss?"

"My Mum's sent a rice pudding for him. She was given a little extra milk from the farm this week and was pleased to make it."

"Are you going to see him? Mum's got lots of little ones, so she can't take it round herself. Could you take it to him, please?"

"Oh, that is kind, Marion." Hetty took the pudding from her carefully.

"Do thank your mother. I've been meaning to pop round to see how he is, so I'll take it with me tonight."

Hetty hadn't been to David's house before, although she knew roughly where it was and that he lived with his widowed mother. Mrs Williams gave her the exact address.

"I'll call round now on my way home. We can't have this rice pudding sitting at school over night after all the trouble Marion's mother has gone to."

She found the house easily. It was a detached cottage at the end of a street made up mainly of terraced houses. There was a hedge in front of it, screening it slightly, with ivy creeping up the wall.

Hetty knocked.

Mrs Holman came to the door. She looked flushed and slightly harassed, not really keen to see a visitor. David had said that she worked part-time at an old people's home.

Hetty explained who she was and why she was there.

Maureen Holman's face relaxed.

"Oh, how kind that girl's mother is. I see her at the women's institute meetings and we often have a good natter together."

"Would you like to come in, my dear? David's still very weak, but I'm sure the sight of your face will cheer him up. He's told me what a help you've been with so many things."

She led the way upstairs.

David was lying back against the pillows listening to the radio. *He still looked terrible,* thought Hetty. His pallor and his laboured breathing told their own story.

But his eyes lit up as he saw her and a faint flush of pleasure came to his cheek. His mother's sharp eyes noticed this.

"I'll leave you two to talk a minute," she said, backing out of the room.

"I won't stay long. Mary will have exhausted my mother-in-law by now, and I must get back to them."

"She's such a happy child, isn't she? I saw her with your mother-in-law the other day. You must be proud of her."

Hetty smiled and turned to David. Fred Astaire's voice was softly filling the room, singing, "Just the way you looked tonight." David went to turn it off.

"Please don't turn it off for me. I love his songs."

"So do I, particularly this one."

"I've been enjoying myself tremendously in your absence." Hetty was enthusiastic.

"Did you know that Mrs Williams had asked me to help while you were away?"

"No," David sounded rather surprised.

"What's she getting you to do then?"

"Well, your class has been divided up amongst the others, as I expect you realise.

"What I'm doing is to take some out of each class to teach them sewing and knitting—and sometimes painting."

"That will be such a help." David was visibly relieved.

"It is so difficult having extra children in your class and I was getting really worried about being away so long."

"Well you can stop worrying then. It's all under control."

They nattered on comfortably for a few more minutes about this child and that, before Hetty rose to go.

"Don't go yet."

"I'm afraid I must. But I'll come again soon if you'd like me to?"

"That's a silly question to ask." David was smiling. "You know I'd like you to."

He put out a hand to her and she grasped it briefly before turning to leave.

Maureen was waiting at the bottom of the stairs.

"He's been really poorly this time. Worse than usual. When you and I would get a cold, he gets bronchitis, and it frightens us both sometimes."

"I'm sorry." Hetty's face showed her concern.

"It must be very difficult for you. He's lucky he's got you."

"I told him I'd pop back again sometime. Is that all right with you?"

"Of course, it is, my dear." Maureen smiled. "I could see it really cheered him up to see you, so you're bound to do him good."

Hetty visited several more times before David returned to school two weeks later.

Mrs Williams caught up with Hetty as she arrived.

"Don't leave us now. You've been such a help. I know what you already do with David's class, and he'll really need you there for a few days until his strength picks up. But we've all enjoyed having you in our classrooms, so any time you can join us will also be very welcome."

---ooo000ooo---

"I don't know what we're going to do to get the colour back in your cheeks."

A week later, Hetty was saying goodbye to David at the end of school on the Friday evening.

"Well now," he studied her face, "a long walk with you would help. It looks as if it's going to be a lovely weekend and it's not too cold at the moment."

"How about it? It would do Mary good too, and I could always carry her if she gets tired."

Hetty considered for a moment.

"Arnold and Mavis are going to visit some elderly relatives tomorrow afternoon, and Mary and I are not invited as the old man is very fragile and sickly. We could come then if you like."

"Good, that's settled." David was delighted. "Can you manage two o'clock?"

"That's fine."

"Shall I walk round to your house and pick you up?"

Hetty knew that it wouldn't be tactful for David to come to her in-laws' house, even if they weren't there.

"Great. I'll see you then."

Saturday dawned, a fine, clear, bright January day. *Ideal for their walk,* thought Hetty. She didn't like to admit to herself how much she was looking forward to it.

She saw a lot of David these days, but never on his own. There was never time to talk. And Hetty wanted time to talk to him. She liked his sense of humour and the fresh way he made her look at things. He was good with Mary too.

At two o'clock on Saturday, David was well wrapped-up with coat and cap and scarf and they set off at a brisk pace. When Mary's legs got tired, David would give her a piggyback to keep her going. She loved that.

"Don't tire yourself." Hetty was anxious. "I can easily carry her."

"She's as light as a feather, I'm enjoying it."

"Now tell me about yourself. I know about Will. But I don't know what you did for a living before you were married or about your family—or about you, yourself, and what you hope to get out of life."

It wasn't difficult to keep him amused with stories of her time working in the dress shop and about her parents and her sister.

"It sounds as if as the younger daughter you were rather spoiled."

Hetty giggled.

"That's what my sister says. I don't know why my parents always blamed her for my misdemeanours, but they did. I suppose it's because I'm quite a lot younger than she is.

"But enough of me, tell me about yourself. I know your mother is a widow. What happened to your father? And have you got a girlfriend hidden away somewhere?"

David smiled ruefully and was silent for a moment and then spoke slowly.

"I'm afraid none of this is very easy to talk about. In fact, I don't think I have ever really talked about any of it."

Hetty looked concerned.

"I'm sorry, it was only a conversational question. Please don't feel you've got to answer it. I shall quite understand. I do know how difficult it can be."

"No, it's time I talked about it and I can't think of anyone I'd rather talk to."

There was silence for a moment. Then David lifted Mary down off his shoulders to give himself time to think.

"You see," he went on, "I would have been married by now if it hadn't been for Ruth's accident..."

"I didn't realise there was a tragedy. How terrible for you. Ruth was your girlfriend, was she?"

"Yes, Ruth was my childhood sweetheart. We, neither of us, ever looked at anyone else and planned to get married just as soon as we were old enough and had enough money put by. We did everything together."

"What happened?" Hetty was concerned at the sadness in David's eyes.

"She had an accident, a bicycle accident. She was on her way to see her grandmother in Wells and cycling as usual when her brakes failed on a hill.

"She obviously fought hard to control the bike, but there were some people walking on the hill and she had just swerved out of control to avoid them when a milk lorry came round the corner and she smashed right into it. The driver could do nothing.

"The walkers tried to revive her and lifted her carefully into the lorry so that the driver could take her to hospital—but she was dead on arrival. There was nothing they could do."

"How dreadful." Hetty was horrified.

"Yes, it was." David ran his hands through his hair. "It was all my fault too."

"What on earth do you mean?"

"I should have checked her brakes for her. I knew she was scatty about looking after things like that, and I should have done it. But I didn't, of course, and I feel so guilty about it."

There was a long silence.

"I'm sorry. I didn't mean all that to come out. It was nearly five years ago now. The trouble is that I've never really talked about it to anyone."

"My mother was still grieving for my father when it happened. He died of cancer when he was only in his mid-fifties. She had been so fond of Ruth too. She was like a daughter to her—the daughter she never had. So I couldn't double her grief by spilling mine out onto her as well."

"Now I think we should have talked," he was thoughtful. "Instead we both bottled our grief up and almost behaved as though nothing had happened. Hopeless!"

"I needed someone like you around to talk to or a brother or a sister. Most of our contemporaries had moved away by then."

"You should have talked about it," Hetty spoke from experience.

"I couldn't have managed without my sister to talk to when the telegram about Will came. She saved me from feeling isolated by my sadness.

"For the first week or two I didn't know how to bring myself to go on looking after Mary. Then Peggy asked me to go and stay with her for a few days, and that helped a lot.

"My parents were kind too, but it's so easy to feel that you are slipping back into the parent-child role that you have left behind and that somehow makes it worse, as if you're denying that you have ever grown up and left home and got married.

"Somebody your own age somehow helps you to face the grief better.

"And, of course, we were Methodists, and they were very kind too, so I had loving people around me both at home and at church and that made a lot of difference.

"I found out that plenty of other people had troubles far worse than mine and that they needed my love and friendship. That helped."

"What you forget in your grief is that you still need to give love as well as receive it. I soon learnt that I wasn't the only one coping with sadness. Nearly everyone has to, one way or another, especially in a war I suppose."

Hetty reached up impulsively and kissed him on the cheek.

"We all face these things in different ways. I think you've done very well too, and I'm so proud you've felt able to tell me about it."

David caught her hand and gave it a squeeze.

"I think you're marvellous the way you've managed. I'm a dismal failure by comparison."

Their eyes met and they would have stood just looking at each other had Mary not noticed an early lamb in a nearby field that she wanted to get to in a hurry.

"Come on." David swung her up onto his shoulders again and jogged across the field to see it.

"You'll spoil her if you carry her too much." Hetty followed, laughing.

"I think we should be getting back soon. It won't be long before the daylight fades now and it already feels a little colder."

David put Mary down and swinging her between them, they turned around and walked home, chatting comfortably about this and that.

She was on his shoulders again when Hetty put her arm through his to help him down a rough bank with his load.

He smiled down at her. "That feels good. Don't move away again. Leave your arm there."

Then, as he turned to leave them, he stopped briefly to kiss them as he waved goodbye.

---ooo000ooo---

It was two days later that he gave her a letter as she was leaving school having done her stint with his class.

"Take that away and read it carefully and privately and think about it." He turned to go.

"That sounds very mysterious," Hetty laughed but then stopped when she saw how embarrassed he looked.

She waited until Mary was asleep and Mavis and Arnold had also gone to bed and then opened the letter.

My dearest Hetty,

I can't stop thinking about that wonderful walk we had together and what fun it was and how close we felt. At least I felt close to you and I can't help wondering whether you felt the same way. In fact, I've been thinking about all we said to each other so much that I thought it might help if I wrote to you about it. I do hope you don't mind.

You see, I discovered the other day that you are not only beautiful and gifted, but you are also wise. You said, 'What you forget in your grief is that you still need to give love as well as receive it', and your words went straight to my heart. I had somehow selfishly locked all my emotions up in a box and thrown away the key. You've helped me unlock the box again and for that I will always be grateful, whatever your reply to this letter.

And talking about emotions, that wonderful walk together, also made me realise that I love you and am wondering whether in any small way you feel the same about me? I know that by rights I shouldn't have mentioned this at the moment, because of Will, and you may still be totally committed to him in your heart. If that is the case I shall quite understand.

But my darling, the future is always unknown and is even more precarious than usual in wartime. As you talked the other day, I found myself wishing that Ruth and I had got married earlier. I can't think why we let ourselves be influenced by all the village conventions and family taboos. We could have had some time together.

I don't want to make the same mistake twice and that's why I am writing. Will you allow me, at least, to declare my love to you and to try to make you happy—even though we know that we may never be able to marry? Must time, or lack of it, limit loving?

Don't you think perhaps that love is God-given in all its forms and that it should never be kept selfishly to oneself but always shared in some way? Isn't that partly what you were saying the other day?

A relationship doesn't have to be physical. It can just be loving and caring, I suppose, although I can't tell you how much I long to hold you in my arms.

Please think about this with all the love and generosity I know you possess. It's your own words that have given me the courage to write.

David

Hetty read it several times and she was thrilled by it and dismayed by it and confused by it, all at once. Sleep wouldn't come and she lay on her back for long hours trying to face its implications and possible complications and weigh them against the feelings she had already begun to acknowledge secretly to herself.

Oh, if only Peggy were here for her to confide in. She needed her help so badly.

It wasn't fair of David to do this to her. Why did he have to write? Why couldn't they have just gone on being ordinary friends the way they were? Had she really encouraged him?

She enjoyed his company enormously and was pleased when Mrs Williams had invited her to go on helping at the school, so that she could see him every day.

Apart from the youngsters in the youth club, he was the only person of about her own age that she had met since she had come to Somerset.

Although Mavis was kind, it was David's friendship that had made all the difference to her stay.

But did she love him?

Did she still love Will, for that matter?

It was here that the confusion lay. David and Will were so different.

Will had been the life and soul of the youth club where they met in Peckham. She had been so flattered when he had singled her out to be his girlfriend and she had enjoyed the romance and excitement of their short time together.

But did Will really love her? He had never written her a love letter. He would telephone her once a week after he had been called up, but that was all. Hetty couldn't really remember him ever saying that he loved her—it was all somehow taken for granted—but she supposed he must have done.

She couldn't remember ever really talking to him either. They hadn't discussed things. She had never felt that she could talk to him about what really mattered to her, as she did with David.

David said he enjoyed talking to her. He thought she was wise!

And yet it was he who made her think and encouraged her to put her thoughts into words and really listened to her. Somehow, he had made her believe in herself as a person.

She had come to depend on him and his company and yes, she admitted, she was beginning to love him. Certainly, she wanted to be with him all the time. He was the one person who could make her laugh.

Most importantly, she didn't want to think of life without him.

But he longed to take her in his arms! She didn't dare think about that. She mustn't let herself be swept off her feet. But on the other hand, she didn't want to lose him either. What a dilemma!

Some girls did have affairs while their husbands and boyfriends were away in the forces. Hetty knew that. But she wasn't that sort of girl. She had always thought that that was a despicable thing to do.

Surely David must think this too.

But what if Will was really dead? What then?

There had been no word for 18 months now—as long again as they had known each other and been married. She found that she had already forgotten some things about him and romanticised others.

Mary had never known him. And Mary loved David, she knew that.

If she really knew that Will was dead, there would be no problem. There was nothing to stop a widow getting married again—after a reasonable interval of about two years.

But what would Mavis and Arnold feel if she started going out with David now, when they still didn't know what had happened to Will?

As far as they knew at the moment, her contact with David was on the same level as her contact with the other teachers at the school and they wouldn't expect it to become any more.

What would her parents think?

More to the point, what would the folk at the school and the villagers think?

It's no good, she thought. *It can't be done.*

We must go on just as we are at the moment and wait until definite news of Will comes.

Finally, as the clock downstairs was striking two o'clock, she wrote briefly:

Dear David,

I loved your letter and I am so happy that you took the trouble to write to me in this way. It means all the world to me. But we can't even think about it, can we?

We have to remember that Will may come back. We have to remember that I am living with Arnold and Mavis, his parents. It just isn't possible.

I'm so sad too. I have valued our friendship so much. Can't we continue as we were or will it be too painful for you? Please say that we can still be friends.

Hetty

She was desperately pale and avoided David's eyes as she gave him her letter the next day and that told him all he needed to know before he even opened it.

He caught her hand as she turned to go.

"I'm sorry. Forget my letter. I should never have written. Please don't stop coming and helping at the school. Let's just continue as we were."

Hetty nodded and walked away quickly, so that he shouldn't see the tears in her eyes.

Somehow, they did manage to resume their friendship over the next few weeks, though now there was always a constraint between them and they took care not to be alone together.

Mavis noticed that her daughter-in-law had lost some of her sparkle.

"Are you all right, dear? You're looking a little tired these days. Are you sure that school isn't taking advantage of you?"

"No, I'm still enjoying it. It's just a long winter, I suppose. I'm longing for a few fine days for a long walk in the sun."

And Mary was looking pale as well.

"Don't take her to school with you today," Mavis was concerned. "She looks so listless that it would never surprise me if she wasn't hatching something."

Mavis was right. Soon Mary was lying like a little waxen doll upon her bed. Her head was burning and her eyes were dull. She couldn't eat and her breathing was laboured.

The doctor looked serious when he examined her.

"It's pneumonia. She's not very old to fight her way through this, so she'll take a lot of nursing. Keep her warm but bathe her with a damp cloth to try to prevent her temperature going up any further.

"Keep giving her sips of water with a little sugar in it too. We mustn't let her become dehydrated. If you can persuade her to take it, a little clear soup would help.

"You must watch her all the time and send for me if there's any change at all. It will be touch and go for quite a long time, I'm afraid."

Hetty's heart sank. What did he really mean? Was she so ill she might die?

Mavis came back from letting the doctor out and saw the expression on Hetty's face.

"It will take time, but she'll be all right, I know she will. I'll take turns with you at night so that you can get some sleep. Don't worry, she's a strong little girl. She'll make it."

Hetty wished that she could have Mavis' confidence.

The two women came closer to each other over the next few weeks as they literally fought for the child's life, taking turns so that she was never alone day or night. They watched her every breath, while the Doctor called daily and usually went away looking grave.

One morning he came in with a smile.

"I have managed to get hold of some of those new wonder pills which have just been given a trial. They're called 'M & B'—don't ask me what that stands for! The trials have been very encouraging though and I think they might be just the thing to help little Mary."

"Well, if you're sure they're all right, Doctor." Mavis wasn't sure.

"I'm sure they will be." Hetty was ready to try anything. "Thank you so much doctor. Shall we start them straight away?"

One pill three times a day was the dose, but it wasn't until the evening of the third day that Mary began to show any improvement. Hetty could feel that she was a little cooler and she managed a sip or two of some clear soup before she fell asleep.

Hetty sat up with her until two am as usual, noticing that at last the child was less restless and appeared to be sleeping more normally.

She smiled when Mavis put her head round the door to take over from her.

"I think she's going to be all right," But the moment the words were out she found herself sobbing.

Mavis put her arm round her.

"Go and make yourself a warm drink and get some sleep. You are going to need more energy tomorrow to keep her amused if she is feeling a little better."

And Mavis was right. Mary was impossible the next day. She appeared much better but was restless and whined all day and they could do nothing to please her.

Then at four o'clock there was a knock at the door.

"That's strange. I wonder who it is. The doctor's been already."

Mavis opened the door and there was David.

"Good evening, Mrs Thomas. The children at the school were so sad to hear how ill little Mary has been that they have drawn lots of pictures for her.

"Hetty's help at the school has been sorely missed—and not least because the older girls enjoyed looking after Mary so much. As you will see, they've even used some of the skills Hetty taught them and made her a rag doll, together with several sets of clothes."

Mavis was amazed.

"How kind of them. Do come in Mr Holman. I'll call Hetty and tell her you're here. I don't know whether it would be wise for you to go in to see Mary yet, just in case there are any infections hanging around at the school."

Hetty's heart lifted at the sight of David and the gifts from the children.

"She is at last a little better, but that means that she's tearful and difficult to please and Mavis and I have been at our wits' end today to try to keep her happy. These things will make all the difference."

David called again a few days later and this time was allowed to see Mary. She was delighted to see him and had drawn him some pictures of the rag doll the children had given her for him to take back to her friends at the school.

He soon became a welcome visitor, always with some little present for Mary from the school children and plenty of stories to make her smile.

Hetty felt her heart go out to him in gratitude.

He in his turn noticed how very tired and drawn she looked and worried about her.

Next time he called; he took Mavis on one side as he was leaving.

"I couldn't help noticing how tired and poorly Hetty looks. If you think a breath of fresh air would help her, I could try to persuade her to come for a walk sometime. What do you think?"

Mavis beamed.

"I think that's a lovely idea. We stopped taking turns to sit up with Mary at night some time ago, but I know that Hetty still doesn't get much sleep as Mary often wakes and I hear her grizzling for this or that."

"Tomorrow's Saturday. So if it is a fine afternoon, I'll call round after lunch if that's all right?"

"Yes, that would be lovely. I'll tell Hetty to expect you and persuade her that it would be good for her to get out. You are kind, and you've been a real friend to us."

---ooo000ooo---

And Saturday was fine with a little strength in the sun.

Hetty was surprised that David had called on a Saturday and even more surprised when Mavis told her why.

"Now you go and get your coat on, dear. It will do you good to get out. You've not moved from this bedroom for about three weeks now and you need the fresh air."

Hetty opened her mouth to protest, but Mavis forestalled her.

"I've got a new game to play with Mary this afternoon. It's a game for two."

Mavis spoke pointedly as she held out her coat to her.

Hetty smiled.

"You win. Thank you so much Mavis."

Without Mary's little legs to hinder them, David and Hetty walked briskly. The village was in the foothills of the Mendips, so there were plenty of lovely routes for them to take.

"Let's see if we can get to Wookey Caves. You haven't seen them, have you? They're well-worth seeing, and much quieter than the caves in Cheddar Gorge, though you must see those sometime as well."

They walked companionably, admiring the view and enjoying the sunshine, the turf of the hills springy under their feet.

The air was stimulating but not too cold, thought Hetty, as she breathed it in gratefully.

They were out of breath as they reached a plateau. There was a small cave behind them, which they poked their noses into before sitting down gratefully for a minute on the flat rock outside it to admire the stunning view.

"Thank you, David. You've been so kind. Your visits to Mary have made all the difference to her. It's such a relief to see her looking so much better," Hetty spoke quietly.

David smiled and held her eyes for a moment.

"My next aim is to see you looking better too. You've lost your sparkle, and that's very important to me.

"I can't bear to see you looking so sad, either. I've been kicking and kicking myself for writing that letter to you. It just wasn't fair of me, I'm so sorry."

"It's all right."

Hetty mumbled and was unable to hold his gaze. She choked back a sob quietly, but suddenly her face was wet with tears and she couldn't stop them.

"Hey, what's this? What a fool I am, I shouldn't have said anything. O Hetty, please don't cry. I can't bear it. I love you so much. I wouldn't hurt you for the world. I can't bear to see you so unhappy. Please, please don't cry."

He handed her his handkerchief as he spoke, but his concern released the floodgates and she sobbed even more so that his handkerchief was soon sodden with her tears.

He sat with his arm round her for some time, just holding her, but she was still sobbing.

Finally, in desperation, he pulled her to her feet and put his arms around her, using the entrance of the cave to shield them at the same time.

"Come on now," he was almost crying himself. "You can't go on crying like this."

"I love you, Hetty. Please, please tell me why you're crying. Please, please tell me what's the matter?"

"I can't bear it. At last she managed to get some words out.

"As if it wasn't enough that I've lost Will, and lost you, I nearly lost Mary as well. I can't bear it."

David pulled her closer.

"What do you mean? What do you mean that you've lost me? You're not thinking straight."

"You don't know that you've lost Will, and you do know that Mary is going to be all right—and as for me, you certainly haven't lost me and you're not going to lose me, I can promise you that."

"No, you can't. If Will came back, I'd have to go back to him, wouldn't I? And then I'd lose you. Then you'd stop loving me."

"Will coming back wouldn't stop me loving you. I shall never stop loving you even if you have to return to him. That's why I wrote to you. I just wanted you to know that I love you."

"I wanted you to be able to remember always, whatever happens, how much I love you… Even if you don't love me," His final words were soft and sad.

Hetty heard them in spite of her sobs.

"Of course, I love you. You must know that."

And now as her sobs still wracked her, she clung to him, lifting her wet face to his and kissing his face, until he began to kiss her in return, her forehead, her eyes and finally her lips.

She didn't pull away but responded passionately, if wetly, as tears still poured down her cheeks.

He released her tenderly for a moment and looked into her eyes.

"Please, don't stop."

"Please…"

She was sobbing and trembling uncontrollably and still clinging to him as if she would never let him go.

He took her further into the cave and laid her on his coat, lying down beside her to hold her even closer.

But still she was sobbing and trembling and kissing was not enough, she wanted more and more.

"I love you," she sounded heartbroken. "I love you so much. Please don't let me go…ever."

"Hetty, I promise I'll never let you go."

He was still desperately trying to calm her.

Then as she started to pull off his jacket and undo his shirt to bury her wet face on his chest, he realised that there was only one way to convince her that he meant what he said. He pulled up her jumper to kiss her breasts and started stroking her hair.

Her tweed skirt had already ridden up exposing her beautiful legs which were the next to be kissed as she tugged at the buttons on his trousers.

"Oh, Hetty. Do you really want this? You know that I do…"

"Of course, of course! Please, please… I want to kiss you there to show you how much I love you."

And so, they gave themselves to each other and in the giving and receiving, her tears were stemmed at last.

---ooo000ooo---

Hetty recovered first.

"I'm so sorry. I'm terrible when I start crying. I just couldn't stop. I shouldn't have done that, but somehow, I couldn't stop myself. It was my fault."

David hugged her.

"I thought it was something we did together, so why do we have to have words like 'my fault'?"

They were brushing their clothes off and standing up as they spoke.

"Hetty, it was wonderful." He pulled her to him again.

"You know it was. Please don't regret it. Didn't I manage to persuade you that I love you? That's what I was trying to do."

She blushed.

"Of course, you did. It's just…it's just…it's so difficult that it's happened now."

"I know." He hadn't meant it to happen either, but he wasn't going to tell her that.

"I'm sorry, Hetty, I'm sorry if I've made it more difficult for you. But I'm not sorry in any other way. How can anyone regret something magical like that, when someone is telling you that they love you? I'm not going to regret it."

His voice was quiet and thoughtful but there was determination behind it.

"I love you and I've discovered that you love me. It's a wonderful gift and something that nobody can take away from us. Thank you, my dearest Hetty, thank you for your generosity and for making me so happy."

"Thank you too." She reached up and kissed him softly. "But…"

David forestalled her, smiling and stroking her hair back from her face.

"No buts. Promise me, promise me, my love, that you won't say 'but' again, that you won't regret what we've done. I can bear anything else, but I can't bear that—now or ever.

"Please promise me," It was an urgent request.

"I promise," Hetty's voice was soft as she looked away embarrassed.

"I shan't know if you mean it unless you look at me."

"I promise," Hetty drew strength from his eyes as she said it.

They walked on companionably together then, hand in hand but not speaking, both busy with their thoughts about the consequences of what they had done.

Finally, David spoke.

"We'd better work out the practicalities of loving each other, I suppose. You know that if you were free, I would ask you to marry me here and now, don't you?"

"I know you would."

Yes, she did know that, she thought, *but it was irrelevant, wasn't it?* They could do nothing in the present circumstances as she had said in her letter.

And yet…they had done something and that had somehow changed everything.

"If you were free and I did ask you, what would your answer be?"

David was still following his line of thought.

"If I was sure you weren't asking me because of what has just happened, I would say yes. But I would have to be sure. I couldn't bear it if you were just asking me out of a sense of duty or pity."

"Oh."

David was taken aback and looked hurt.

"What on earth makes you think that I would want to marry you out of duty or pity, when I've been trying so hard to persuade you that I love you?"

His hurt made him sound almost angry.

Hetty was satisfied.

"I love you too and if you asked me to marry you, I would be very proud and I would say yes."

And this answer meant, of course, that David had to stop and kiss her again.

---ooo000ooo---

"We were talking about practicalities before that diversion. What on earth do we do next?"

"I don't see that we can do anything. We don't know if Will is really dead, so we can't do anything."

"You're right. For the sake of Mavis and Arnold alone— quite apart from the school authorities—we can't do the natural thing and let other people know that we love each other."

"I think we'll just have to go on as we have been," Hetty's voice was sad.

"I suppose you're right. For the time being, at least, we'll probably have to be content with the occasional opportunities like this that come our way and make the most of them.

"We're lucky that we see each other every day at the school and even though that will be somewhat frustrating now, we must make it count creatively without drawing attention to ourselves. Together we'll cope somehow."

Hetty was satisfied.

"You're right. That's what we must do, however hard it is."

And suddenly because David had used the word 'together' the world seemed a better place and full of hope again.

She grabbed his hand and kissed it.

"I love you."

"And I love you too." He held onto her hand.

"And now we must get up to those main caves, so that Mavis and Arnold are not suspicious when we get back."

Hetty laughed.

"Yes, but perhaps you'd better just tell me all about them so that I can sound convincing. Somehow I don't think we're going to make the full walk now and get back in time."

And so, David told her all about them, as they made their way back, while Hetty searched the hedgerows for the one or two blackberries that could still be found.

---ooo000ooo---

Life went on as usual for about six weeks for David and Hetty. Not able to acknowledge their love in public, they had to be content with seeing each other every day and very little else. Whenever possible, a loving look would pass between them, emphasising their togetherness, and the odd snatched conversation at school or at the youth club was a bonus. It was frustrating to say the least.

Then the morning sickness started.

Hetty had wondered why she was feeling so tired and listless. Now she knew. What was she to do? How could she go to the local doctor?

What about Mavis and Arnold? What about her work at the school? What about the youth club? How could she tell David? She never had a moment with him alone. He had told her she was never to regret making love with him. That was going to be a tall order!

The morning sickness had been going on for about a week, when Mavis, who was sitting at the kitchen table while Hetty cleared the breakfast things, said slowly.

"You know, Hetty, how fond I am of you. We've grown so close over the past few months, haven't we?"

Then she added softly, looking at the table.

"But if you're going to be poorly, I really think that perhaps it would be better if you braved the air-raids in London and went home to your Mother. As you know Arnold is not very good with poorly people."

So she's guessed, thought Hetty.

"I've wondered about that too. I'll write to my Mother today."

"I'm so sorry, Mavis, I don't know what to say."

And the tears sprang to her eyes and began to trickle down her cheeks.

"Don't say anything," Mavis spoke quickly and Hetty noticed she was also crying.

"I don't want to know anything. What I do want is for us to be able to continue as friends. And, of course, above all else I want to be able to continue my contact with my lovely little granddaughter, Mary. I'm sure you'll understand that."

"Yes, of course. That goes without saying. And Mary is so very fond of you too. She'll miss you when we go. I'll leave her with you for a few minutes while I go and write if that's all right."

"Yes, of course it is, my dear," Mavis called Mary over to come and help her to make some jam tarts.

Hetty went to her bedroom and wrote two letters. The first was brief and to the point.

Dear David,

I have been feeling very tired and low for some time now and then about a week ago, I started being sick every morning and I guessed what had happened. I'm expecting a baby! And this morning, Mavis indicated that she had guessed too, and suggested that if I was going to be 'poorly' it would be better if I braved the bombs and went home to my Mother. She was so nice and tactful, I'm afraid I cried. She was crying too and said she didn't want to know anything but that Arnold wasn't very good with 'poorly' people and, of course, she's right. I told her that I would write to my parents straight away. In fact, that's what I'm meant to be doing at the moment.

My parents love me, but they will be horrified. I can't think for a minute that they will really want me home although they will try to be kind. My letter to them will already be in the post by the time you read this, as I will put it in the box on my way to school this afternoon.

I am holding hard onto your 'no buts' and my promise not to have any regrets, and I can't be sad that I'm having your baby, because I love you, but we are in a quandary. If the worst comes to the worst, perhaps my sister would help, but I can't really expect her to. She will be shocked too!

Don't worry, I'm not expecting anything from you except love and advice.

In haste, Hetty

The letter to her parents was more difficult. Perhaps it would be easier if it just went to her mother in the first instance. Then she knew her mother would be tactful in the way she broke the news to her father.

Dear Mum,

I don't know an easy way to tell you this. Please, please don't be too angry and shocked and upset.

You will remember that I've told you in previous letters that I help with the Methodist Church Youth Fellowship and about David, the leader. He's such a nice person and, as I've told you, I help at the school where he works too.

Well, that time that Mary was so seriously ill with pneumonia, Mavis persuaded me to get a break and go for a walk with him, while she sat with Mary, who was just beginning to get better. She had got to know him as he had brought presents from the youth club girls and the school children for Mary several times and had been so kind.

We've got to know each other well over the months and he's become a real friend. There are hardly any other young people in the village, of course. They've all been called up.

But as a schoolteacher, David hasn't had to go yet, and anyway he gets bad asthma so they may not want him.

He's told me about some unhappy times in his life and I've told him about Will. His childhood sweetheart, whom he had hoped to marry, was killed in an accident.

It was a lovely autumn day when we started out but I was exhausted and upset that Mary had been so ill—as you know we very nearly lost her—and I was finding that very difficult to bear, especially as we still don't know what's happened to Will.

Well, suddenly David noticed that I was crying. I didn't mean to, but it just happened. And once I'd started I couldn't stop—you know what I'm like. I was in a hopeless state.

He talked to me to start with and tried to dry my tears, but I couldn't stop and he was getting desperate about it and started pleading with me to stop because he loved me. I knew this anyway, as some time ago he sent me a sweet letter to say so, because he thought it would help me to know that somebody loved me in my forlorn state at the moment and that it would be something for me to hang on to if Will never does return.

But, of course, I had written back saying that I would value his friendship but nothing more and we had both agreed on that.

And then on the walk, with me crying my eyes out and totally unable to stop, and quite without either of us meaning to do it, we were overwhelmed by our love for each other and made love. And it was—it is—love, Mum. Really it is. And you will have guessed the rest. We made love just that one time, but yes, I'm expecting a baby, due next October I should think.

Mavis noticed my early morning sickness this morning and though not saying that she had guessed what was the matter, she said that she thought that if I was going to be poorly, it would be a good idea for me to come home to you and I, of course, agreed and said that I would write to you.

I haven't had a chance to tell David yet but I will put a note in his hand at the school today, explaining what has happened. I know he loves me and that he will be kind and supportive. That is the sort of person he is. I also know that if we ever hear that poor Will is really dead, then he wants to marry me, because he has told me so.

But of course, we can't marry until we know definitely what has happened to Will—even though I feel sure he must really be dead as it is 18 months now since I got that terrible telegram.

And now, I hardly dare to ask it, but can I come home until the baby arrives? I'm so very, very sorry to be such a nuisance, and as soon as the baby is born, I will find a way of supporting myself. Please say yes.

From your ever-loving daughter,
Hetty

---ooo000ooo---

Hetty was due to help at the school that afternoon and arriving a little early at the end of the lunch break, she noticed that David was still on duty in the playground. Quickly giving her letter to Mary, she told her to run across and give it to David, thinking that it would be less noticeable than if she gave it to him herself.

"Thank you, Mary," David smiled down at her as she gave it to him. "You make a very good post-girl."

He read the letter mid-afternoon, after he'd set his class the task of writing a story. He was shell-shocked for a moment, but then a deep joy overwhelmed him.

His child… Hetty was having his child. How wonderful! He'd always wanted a child. He loved children. But it would be difficult.

I must think carefully about what to do for the best, he thought. *Hetty must be so worried.*

Then a stifled giggle from two of his class who looked as if they were playing 'cat's cradle' beneath the desks, made him look up as they furtively hid the string away.

He pretended not to notice but got up and gradually moved round the room with a comment here and a suggestion there as to how each story should proceed.

"You're looking very happy, sir," said Eileen Harris, one of the girls. "Is it your birthday?"

David laughed. "No, not my birthday, Eileen, but I am very pleased about something."

"What's that, sir," she persisted.

"My, you are a nosey parker," he said. "Mind your own business and get on with your work."

But he said it kindly and she knew he was not really cross as she bent to redouble her efforts to make her story good enough to please him.

Hetty was with Mrs Williams' class that afternoon but put her head round his door as usual before she left, just in case he was free of children and could talk for a minute.

Her heart thumped as she opened the door. What would he think! Supposing she was wrong about him! Supposing he was upset!

She needn't have worried. For once David was on his own in an empty room and the last child who was leaving called out to her.

"He's in ever such a good mood today, Miss. He's very pleased about something."

Hetty smiled and walked over to David.

"Have you had time to read my letter? I'm sorry to spring such news on you at school, but I didn't know what else to do."

"Of course, I've read your letter. Didn't you hear Eileen say I was in a good mood? I'm so thrilled I just can't keep the smile off my face. I've always wanted a child."

"But not like this…"

Hetty nevertheless couldn't help smiling back at him. His enthusiasm was infectious and filled her with hope. The togetherness he had spoken about on their walk was working. Perhaps it would be all right. Perhaps it could all work out so that nobody got too badly hurt. She did hope so.

"Not another 'but' surely." David was laughing.

"Our baby is not going to be an inconvenience. It's going to be wanted and loved. We'll just have to put some hard work into thinking how to organise everything, that's all."

"Today's Friday, so I'll put my thinking cap on over the weekend."

"You can't go on staying with Mavis and Arnold, of course, and I certainly don't want you to go back to your parents if they are going to be as horrified as you think."

"I know," David was thoughtful.

"As Mavis has already guessed, she's not going to mind if I take you out for a walk again on Saturday afternoon. Don't say anything. I'll just turn up."

"OK."

Hetty, turned to go, aware that Mrs Williams or one of the other teachers could come in at any minute.

"I'll expect you. Come on Mary, we're going now."

"And remember, I like the patter of tiny feet." David was laughing.

"What does he mean that he likes tiny feet?" asked Mary.

"He means that he likes your little feet," Hetty was laughing too.

"Has anyone ever told you that you are beautiful when you laugh?"

Hetty made an exasperated sound and left quickly, but she was still laughing.

---ooo000ooo---

David thought hard all the way home, trying to work out a plan of action.

Hetty couldn't stay with Mavis and Arnold—and she couldn't stay in the village at all for that matter. The village folk knew about Will.

At the moment everyone loved her for the way she was helping with the youth club and at the school. But David knew that as soon as the first gossip found out about the baby, the whole population would turn on her and make her life impossible.

His position would be very difficult too. He was not going to deny that he was the baby's father. In fact, he had already made up his mind to tell his mother when he got home that night.

But village folk didn't like their unmarried schoolteachers to have babies and unless he and Hetty were very careful there would be a scandal and he would probably be asked to resign. The same thing would happen at the Methodist Youth Club.

As Hetty had said in her letter, it was a quandary. What a dear girl she was. She had said that she was *pleased* to be having his baby. The thought thrilled him once again.

He forced his mind back to the problem of what to do.

Hetty would have to leave the village and move somewhere more anonymous like Wells. He would have to find her a home there.

His friend, John, had worked at Wells Primary School before he was called up and David quite often spent an evening with his wife, Penny, to cheer her up now he was away from home.

She would be discreet, he was sure, if he told her what had happened. Perhaps she would know of somewhere that Hetty could go. They had children, so Mary wouldn't miss her friends in the village so much if she could play with them.

It was important that Hetty got the proper medical care too—and the sooner, the better.

But what excuse could be made for her leaving the village if she wasn't going back to her parents?

And she'd be lonely. Even if he got to see her nearly every evening, she'd still be lonely during the day. He didn't like the thought of it.

But his first task was to tell his mother.

---ooo000ooo---

Maureen was not impressed with the news he gave her.

"Oh David, surely you could have taken more care of her than that. She is such a lovely girl and she still has a husband, for goodness sake. How could you do it?"

"Mother, of course I understand why you're angry," David spoke gently.

"I'm angry with myself too in a way, although I can't and won't regret it because although we had agreed just to be friends, we really love each other.

"And I'm sorry, but I cannot be anything but thrilled about the child. I've always wanted a baby—and I thought that you would be pleased at the thought of a grandchild."

"Of course, I'm pleased at the thought of a grandchild. But not like this. Not a hole-in-the-corner affair like this. Oh David, what were you thinking of?"

"It wasn't like that, Mother. We love each other. I've loved Hetty ever since she arrived in the village, as you may have guessed.

"She was upset because Mary had been so ill and I gave her a hug and it somehow got out of hand and we went too far. It was not her fault. She was so distressed and that seemed to be the only way to comfort her."

"Some comfort. Out of the frying pan into the fire."

David was annoyed.

"Don't be like that. I wouldn't have told you at all if I'd thought you'd be like that.

"I love Hetty and want to marry her—and if poor Will really is dead as the telegram said, then as soon as that's confirmed, we will get married.

"Hetty is a lovely girl and I can't believe my luck that she feels the same way about me. She had that telegram about Will nearly two years ago now, you know."

Maureen sighed, despairingly.

"I know she's a lovely girl and little Mary is a beautiful child whose grandparents, Arnold and Mavis, are not going to be happy about this. And Will was a lovely lad too and may well not be dead."

"That's why I've come to you, Mother. Hetty has written to her parents to see if she can go home to have the baby—but I don't like the idea of that solution, as she has said that she knows they will be horrified.

"I think that if I can find her some lodgings somewhere near John and Penny in Wells, that might be far enough away for people here not to find out.

"We must think out a feasible reason for her to go there— one that people will accept as quite natural. With John away in the army, Penny is pretty lonely too."

"That will work as long as nobody from the village bumps into her in Wells and notices that she is 'expecting'."

"I know, I would hate her to become the object of gossip or scandal, but I think we may have to risk that. I want her near enough so that I can get over to see her most evenings, or it will be so lonely for her."

"Has she no friend who would come and live with her or a sister, perhaps. I think you said that she had a sister?"

"That's right. She has got a sister, and the sister has two children so it would be fairly natural for them to come down this way to get away from the bombing.

"Well done, Mother, I'll suggest that to her."

"Poor Hetty. She must be terribly distressed. Do tell her to come and talk to me if she wants to."

"That's kind of you, Mother. I know you'll love her as you get to know her better."

"I know I will love her. But that's not the point at the moment, is it?"

David was thoughtful.

"No, the most important things are that Hetty and Mary are looked after properly and feel cared for and loved and that the baby, when it arrives, knows that it is loved and wanted as well.

"You may be sure that I'll look after the loving and caring for Hetty, whatever happens. She's had a terrible time. She's still very young. And she's so brave and resourceful. I adore her!"

"I can see you're a hopeless case," Maureen was sighing and half-laughing at the same time. "But I suppose I wouldn't have you any different really."

---ooo000ooo---

59

David was on his bike on the way to Wells early the next morning, arriving at John and Penny's house just as she and the children were finishing breakfast.

"You're on an early visit," Penny said as she opened the door.

"Come on in… The tea's still hot in the pot if you'd like a cuppa. Move up children. Uncle David's come to see us."

"We haven't seen you for ages. This is a nice surprise. Is everything OK?"

"I need your help," David was blunt. He glanced at the children.

"Have you a moment for a private word?"

"Yes, of course. Run along outside now children and have a game in the garden, while I talk to Uncle David."

"That's not fair," Mark, their eldest, was indignant. "We want to talk to him too."

"It'll be your turn later," David promised. "Run along now."

Penny's reaction to David's story wasn't very different to his mother's.

"I didn't think you were that sort of person, David," Penny sounded sarcastic.

"I'm finding all this very hard to believe. Poor girl! What on earth will happen when people in your village find out? She'll be practically lynched. You can't have thought very hard about what you were doing."

David sighed and put his head in his hands.

"I know, I know. But that's why I need your help. You must believe me when I tell you that Hetty and I love each other dearly."

"This wasn't meant to happen. It was just an isolated incident."

"I shall quite understand if you don't feel able to help in any way, but you and John are my oldest friends and I don't know where else to go."

"What do you want me to do then? Of course, we're your friends and of course I will help you. It's just a situation that takes a bit of getting used to, that's all."

"Thank you. I know how it must look to you and I also know what will happen if she stays in the village."

"I am hoping to be able to find her digs here in Wells with somebody who will be sympathetic to her."

"I would also like it to be somewhere near you, so that she has a friend to come to if she needs one."

"Her little girl, Mary, is the same age as your little Margaret, so I thought they might enjoy playing together."

"Am I asking too much? Just tell me, and I'll understand."

Penny sighed but then spoke thoughtfully.

"Of course, you're not asking too much. Any friend of yours is a friend of ours and I'll be pleased to help."

"But as to where she can live, I don't know what to suggest. We haven't got any spare room here. When John's mother comes to stay, she has to sleep in the sitting room."

"I wonder though… I wonder about Mrs Smith, down the road."

"She's only comparatively recently been made a widow. Her husband was a pilot and he was shot down over Germany."

"She didn't have definite news of his death for about three months, so I would think that she would be sympathetic to Hetty—if she will have her, that is."

"She must have plenty of room, though. And I should think she must be pretty lonely. She used to have some evacuees living with her, but they've gone home now."

David breathed a sigh of relief.

"She sounds perfect. I wonder, could you possibly spare the time to come with me to see her and ask her? She doesn't know me, so it would be easier if someone she knows goes to her door."

"What will you tell her?"

"Probably not the truth. What do you think?"

"Just tell her that you have a friend who wants to move down here to get away from the bombing, and that you wondered whether she had any room. I think it's better to be brief in the first instance."

She called to the children.

"Come on. We're going out for a quick walk with David to see Mrs Smith up the road."

The children raced ahead.

Janet Smith answered the door rather nervously but smiled when she saw Penny and the children.

"I haven't seen you for ages. Come on in. Would the children like a drink?"

There was a chorus of "Yes, please."

"Oh, that is kind of you. As you heard they'd love one."

"But before we come in, I must introduce our friend David to you. He's an old friend of John's from college days and sometimes comes across to cheer me up. The children are hoping he'll spend some time playing with them too."

The introductions made, they all trooped into Janet's house and sat round her kitchen table, the children with glasses of orange squash and the adults with cups of tea.

"I hope we're not going to make you short of milk, Janet?" Penny was anxious.

"Don't worry. I enjoy tea just as much without milk, so there isn't a problem."

Penny was grateful.

"Actually, we've come to ask you whether you can help us. The wife of a friend of David's is down here to get away from the bombing in London, and we were wondering whether, now that your evacuees have gone, you would think about renting a room to her? She has a little girl of three and is expecting another child."

Janet Smith looked a bit taken aback for a minute. Then she spoke slowly and thoughtfully,

"I see. I have got the room, I suppose, now that the three little evacuees I had have gone back to London, but I wasn't thinking of taking in any more lodgers."

She turned to Penny.

"She's a friend of yours, is she? We'd obviously need to get on all right at such close quarters."

"I haven't met her yet, but David speaks very highly of her."

Now it was David's turn to speak up.

"She has been staying with Mr and Mrs Thomas in our village and has become a great favourite with everyone. She has been helping at the school and in the youth club too."

"What a pity she can't stay in the village, then." Janet was practical.

"Yes, it is, but as Penny said she is expecting another child and Mr Thomas has made it quite clear that he doesn't like babies. He is getting rather elderly, you see."

"I'm sure you'd like her, Mrs Smith."

"What do you think? Would it be too much for you?"

"Well, I suppose I am rather lonely." Janet Smith responded to his smile.

"But before we arrange anything definite, I wonder if you'd mind bringing her to meet me. It wouldn't be too far for her to come on a visit, would it?"

"That's a good idea, but is this afternoon too early?"

"No, this afternoon is fine. And she has a little girl you say? You'd enjoy playing with her, wouldn't you, Margaret?"

And so it was settled.

---ooo000ooo---

David received a frosty reception from Mavis when he called early afternoon. She didn't invite him in when he asked for Hetty and spoke coldly as he stood on the doorstep.

"I was wondering whether you knew our son, Will? You must have gone to the same school and are about the same age, so I'd have thought you would have known him a bit. He went to the Methodist Church Youth Club too."

"I still can't believe he's dead, you know. I'm sure he'll come back sometime..."

Her voice trailed off.

David felt dreadful but replied quietly.

"I do remember him Mrs Thomas, though unfortunately I never knew him well. He was such a talented boy, wasn't he? Everyone spoke so well of him."

"I'm so sorry, Mrs Thomas. I know how you must feel..."

She turned her heel on him and replied brusquely.

"It doesn't seem like it. I'll call Hetty."

A minute or two later, Hetty was there with Mary at her heels.

"Put your coats on. You and Mary and I are catching the next bus to Wells. Tell Mavis where you're going and that you will be back about six o'clock."

---ooo000ooo---

As soon as she saw Hetty and Mary standing on her doorstep, Janet Smith's heart went out to them. Hetty was very young and the child was lovely. She could do with someone to mother again.

She invited them in and showed Hetty a large front bedroom.

"But I shan't expect you to sit up there all the time. I'd like you to make yourself at home and for you and Mary to become part of the family."

Hetty was both relieved and delighted.

"You're so kind. Has David told you that I am expecting a baby? I wouldn't like it to come as a nasty shock to you!"

"I love babies, don't worry. And no doubt we'll have the proud father down here on compassionate leave when the baby arrives, shall we?"

Hetty blushed and looked awkward. David came to the rescue quickly.

"Hetty's husband is in the Far East at the moment, so I'm afraid she'll have to put up with friends like me and Penny from along the road for the time being."

"When do you want to come, dear? It doesn't matter to me."

Hetty answered slowly,

"Well, I don't want to leave Mavis and Arnold in a hurry, as they have been very kind, and so have many other people in the village.

"So perhaps next Saturday would be all right? That would give me time to say goodbye to the young people at the youth club on Tuesday evening."

And it will also give my parents time to reply to my letter, she thought.

"That's arranged then, dear. I suggest that you arrive in time for lunch so that Mary has time to settle in during the afternoon and perhaps have a game with Margaret, down the road."

"Thank you so much, David." Hetty was grateful as they walked away.

"She's so nice, isn't she? How on earth did you find her?"

"You've got Penny to thank for that. Come and meet her. She lives over there with her two children Tom and Margaret. Her husband John, who is one of my oldest friends, is away in the army."

Penny welcomed them warmly and soon forgot her reservations about Hetty and David's relationship.

I've no right to make judgements, she thought. *I'd be in a terrible state if I'd had a telegram about John saying he was 'Missing, presumed dead'. She can't know whether she's coming or going, poor thing.*

Margaret was busy reading Mary a story when David spoke next.

"Come on, let's all go out and show Mary the cathedral clock, have a cup of tea and a sticky bun and then go and see the swans ringing the bell for their tea in the cathedral close before we walk home."

"Hurray!" shouted the children. "That sounds lovely. Come on Mary."

They excitedly found their coats and boots struggling to get them on as quickly as possible so that no time was lost.

As they walked, David explained to them how many years ago the swans had been taught how to ring the bell, which hung most afternoons at the side of their pool. This normally happened at three in the afternoon and there were always folk watching.

They had a lovely afternoon all together and Mary enjoyed watching the figures on the clock move out when the hour struck. Best of all, though, she loved watching the swans ring the bell for their tea.

"I'll tell Granny about them when we get home. She will laugh."

---ooo000ooo---

Hetty told Mavis about their visit to Janet and Penny in Wells that evening and about the arrangement for her to go to live there in a week's time.

"I think perhaps Peggy, my sister, might want to come down to stay with me to get away from the bombing sometime soon, so perhaps we could say that I am moving into Wells so that we can be together there."

"You're a very lucky girl to have found someone to have you."

"Does she know…?"

"Yes. She likes children, which is just as well as my sister has two."

Then Hetty asked,

"Do you think you'll be able to make the journey to visit us sometimes?"

"I know Mary will miss you dreadfully otherwise—and so will I. You've been so kind to me. I'm sorry things have turned out like this."

"Yes, I'll come." Mavis turned away abruptly so that Hetty shouldn't see her face.

---ooo000ooo---

The letter back to Hetty from her parents did not come until the Friday, but she was very surprised by the contents. Firstly, it was from her father not her mother and then it was almost as if, in what she said to Mavis, she had known what her parents would do.

Dear Hetty,

Your mother cried and cried when she read your letter. She couldn't believe that a daughter of hers would behave as you must have done and, of course, she blamed herself.

She has, in fact, made herself quite poorly over the whole business. How could you do it? How could you do it to yourself, to Mary, to your Mother and to poor Will? I just can't understand it at all. You were always such a good little girl and we had such high hopes of you.

I'm glad you think this chap, David, will take care of you. But I'm afraid you may be sadly disillusioned. Perhaps we have sheltered you too much so that you don't know what some men are like.

I think it's very unlikely that he will do anything for you. Far more likely that he has already walked away from you and is denying the baby is his. If so, I must say that I am sorry for you, even though it is all your own fault. Did you never learn to say no?

But enough of being angry. Your mother was so upset that she spilled the whole sorry story out to Peggy. And Peggy, wonderful girl that she is, insists on coming down to see you and be with you. That made your mother feel a bit better, I can tell you.

Can you look around for somewhere, preferably in the next village or town and not near Mavis and Arnold, where Peggy and Sarah and Peter (they will have to come with her, of course) can stay with you and Mary? This chap, David, ought to help you do that if he does nothing else!

I don't know how I would keep my hands off him if I saw him!

As soon as you've found somewhere write and let Peggy know and they will all come and stay until the baby arrives.

I'm so very angry with you, so very disappointed in you, but I am still your loving,

Father

Hetty cried and cried when she received this letter. Her tears were mostly out of grief that her parents did not begin to understand, but also out of anger at their attitude. How could they be so cruel as to think that a man she loved would be so cheap and nasty as they suggested.

67

But at least Peggy was coming. And the children too. That was wonderful. What a relief. Peggy might be a bit cross too, but she would understand, Hetty was sure of that.

She wouldn't have offered to come otherwise. She would have to look round for somewhere for her to stay too. She wrote:

Dear Peggy,

I can't tell you how grateful I am that you are coming down to see me, and bringing the children too, especially in the circumstances.

I know that Dad thinks that David must be a bad lot, but I can promise you that he isn't. I knew he loved me and that I loved him, but we didn't mean this to happen.

Mary was so very, very ill that we thought she would die, and when she turned the corner and started to get better, Mavis persuaded me that it would do me good to get out and go for a walk with David.

He'd been so kind while she was ill, bringing her letters and pictures from the children at the school and all sorts of things. I was so grateful to him and also still very emotional about Mary having been so ill…it was just one of those things and more my fault than David's really. Do please try to understand.

David has been wonderful and has found me some digs in Wells, as I obviously cannot go on living with Mavis and Arnold in the circumstances.

When I get there, I'll look around for somewhere for you and the children to stay. It will be wonderful to have you.

Love, Hetty

---ooo000ooo---

David noticed how crestfallen she looked when she came to say goodbye to the teachers and pupils at the school but put it down to the goodbyes she was having to say.

"I'll come and help you with your cases tomorrow morning, but I think you'll have to get them to the bus stop on your own, as I'm obviously not welcome at 14 Wells Road…"

"Don't let the goodbyes get you down. Keep smiling, my love. Whatever you do, keep smiling somehow."

The goodbyes to Mavis and Arnold were not easy, especially as Mary clung to Mavis and wanted her to come too. Arnold was easier, but he was obviously rather puzzled as to why she was going just into Wells and couldn't stay with them any longer.

"Come and see us soon," Hetty gave Mavis a last hug.

She was very pleased to see David waiting for them at the bus stop and soon they were joggling and rattling their way to Wells, crammed together in two seats on the bus, with Mary on Hetty's lap, the cases safely stored in the luggage compartment by the door.

"You're very quiet," David was concerned. "I'm so sorry this has been so difficult for you."

Hetty rummaged in her handbag.

"It's not that. Read this." She handed him the letter from her father.

"I see," his voice was grim as he handed it back. "Well, I'm doubly glad you're not going home now."

"But don't let it upset you." He noticed that Hetty was wiping away a silent tear.

"I'm sorry they feel like that, but they really don't understand, do they? Why must people always believe the worst rather than the best?"

"That's what upsets me most. The way they assume you must be a terrible person, when you've been so kind and caring and have taken all the blame on yourself when it was really all my fault for not being able to control my tears."

David nudged her kindly.

"Don't despise your tears, Hetty. It had nothing to do with them. I seem to remember telling you I loved you. If anyone's at fault, it's me for keeping on about loving you."

"And I thought we'd got past the regretting stage. Please don't let your father's letter bring it all back."

"As I told you then, I can bear anything else, but I can't bear that. I thought we were together in this and regrets just separate us."

It was that word 'together' again and once again it comforted Hetty.

She smiled at him.

"You're right, of course. We've got to look forward together now."

"That's right, we have to plan for the future together."

"And that probably means forgetting your father's letter that would tie us to the past and forgetting your parents' hang-ups about what they want for their daughter and the way they think you ought to behave.

"I always saw you as an independent spirit, somebody who thought for herself and that's partly why I fell in love with you. Am I right?"

Hetty smiled.

"Yes, I suppose that's why I was always in hot water as a child. I wanted to do things my way and think out things for myself."

"Well now you have to think your way through this, but you don't have to do it alone anymore. We'll do it together and together we'll cope somehow."

They were quiet for a moment, each thinking their own thoughts, while Mary slept on her mother's lap.

"What's Peggy like? Will it be a help to you if she comes down here to be near you? Will you like that?"

"Oh, yes. Peggy's a dear, really. She can sometimes be a bit grumpy on the surface, but she's a really loving person underneath—and her children, Sarah and Peter are lovely. I'm sure they'd be good for Mary too."

"Well, how about this for a next step then."

"First of all, write to your father and mother. Make it brief, not apologetic but loving and say how pleased you are that Peggy plans to come down and that you are looking out for somewhere and will write again soon."

"Give them your new address and tell them what has happened so far. Again, don't try to explain yourself—or me

—just give them the facts and your love. Does that sound a good idea?"

"Yes, it sounds just right," Hetty gave a sigh of relief.

"Janet Smith's house is a big one," she was thoughtful. "I wonder whether she would have room for them there, as well as me."

"First of all, give yourself a little while to settle in and get to know her and then see if you think it would work before you ask her," David's advice sounded sensible.

---ooo000ooo---

Janet Smith was very welcoming and Hetty soon felt at home and comfortable in her house, while Mary enjoyed going to play with Penny's daughter, Margaret, every day when Margaret got home from school.

It wouldn't be so very long before Mary would be going to school herself and she missed her visits to the village school with Hetty, so it helped to have a daily routine like this.

Hetty usually accompanied her to natter to Penny and to give Janet a little peace on her own without them for a short time, when she came in from her work in a local insurance office.

She told Penny about Peggy and how she would like to come down to Wells too, to look after her when she had the baby.

"Sarah is a little older than Mark and Peter is about a year older than Margaret, so it would be quite a houseful, wherever they go."

"Have you thought of asking Janet? She might have room for them, too."

"Yes, I had thought of it but she is so kind and I don't want to impose on her."

"Well, why don't you just ask her if she knows of anywhere that Peggy can stay, and then it is up to her to offer, or not, as she sees fit."

"Yes, of course, that's a good idea. I'll do it that way."

David, who had insisted on giving Hetty the money for the rent, was a frequent visitor. In fact, he got across after his meal nearly every evening—except Tuesdays—just as Hetty was finishing reading Mary her bedtime story.

Mary was in bed and half-asleep as Hetty was reading to her, which gave David and Hetty a few treasured minutes for some private conversation and a quiet kiss before they went downstairs to be with Janet in the sitting room.

This arrangement had carried on happily for about a month with Hetty and Janet really beginning to enjoy each other's company and get closer to each other when Janet suddenly said to Hetty one evening, just after David had left, "I think that man's in love with you, you know. It stands out a mile."

Hetty blushed.

"I know. He's so very kind too, as you can see. Oh dear, it's so complicated."

"Life is never easy. I believe you said that your husband is in the Far East, is that right? It must be miserable for you."

So Hetty took a deep breath and told her the whole story.

Janet listened sympathetically.

"I know what it feels like to get a telegram which says, '*Missing, presumed dead*'. The same thing happened to me, but there was a second telegram only three months later saying that his body had been found in a remote country district in France, where his plane had come down. He had been trying to limp home to salvage the plane I suppose and hadn't made it. It was completely burnt out when they found it."

"How terrible. I suppose I dread hearing how Will has been killed as much as anything else. It's awful not knowing what's happened, but knowing the worst is just as bad. I'm so sorry."

"You've made me feel that I was lucky to hear so quickly. The suspense has gone on so long now for you that you must almost feel you've forgotten what he looks like."

"I suppose that's partly the trouble. We were married such a short time before he was called up. He's only seen Mary

72

twice, and one of those times was the day after she was born, and I've now got to the stage when I feel I hardly know him—if I ever did."

"And David, well you can see for yourself what David is like. He is so kind and loving and he wants to marry me if Will doesn't come back."

"I hope you're not too shocked. I shall quite understand if you want me to move somewhere else."

"No, no, my dear. Of course, I understand and of course you must stay here."

"I remember one of the worst things when that telegram came to me was that I didn't have a child—I didn't have any little bit of Ernie to hold on to."

"I had wanted a child so desperately badly before he left, but he said that he wanted us to wait till he came home again. I wished so much that I hadn't agreed to that."

"That's partly why I'm enjoying your little Mary so much—and why the new baby will be welcome too."

At this point Hetty told her about Peggy and about how she wanted to come and look after her while she had the baby, bringing her two children with her.

"Do you know anybody who would have her? Her children are very well-behaved, so I don't think there would be any problem and it would only be for the time over the birth."

"Tell her to come here. It sounds a good arrangement as I was a little worried about how you'd cope if the baby decided to arrive during the day while I was out at work."

Another result of this heart to heart, was that Janet now occasionally left David and Hetty alone together in the evening, when she went to a women's institute meeting, while in the summer she would babysit for them while they went for an evening walk.

---ooo000ooo---

73

Hetty enjoyed her new life in Wells—David made sure that she did. He fed her books that he thought she would enjoy and then discussed them with her.

He gave her a wireless and told her when there was good music coming on that she ought to listen to.

He suggested that rather than attend Wells Methodist Church, she should go to the Cathedral Morning Service where she would be more anonymous and sometimes, he would even accompany her to Evensong on Sunday evenings.

Best of all he got to see her as much as he possibly could. He got very fit that summer as the cycle ride to Wells and back took about 40 minutes each way.

Hetty for her part was careful to do her shopping very early in the day, before most folk from the village had had time to get to Wells on the bus. That way they were less likely to bump into her and notice that she was expecting a baby.

It was seldom possible for them to express their love for each other physically because of the constraints of their situation, but their love nevertheless blossomed and grew as they got to know each other better.

David's encounter with Mavis had shaken him badly—especially because of her belief that Will was still alive.

Although he and Hetty longed to be living together as husband and wife, they were both now quite sure they shouldn't do so until they knew that Will was really dead—and in the event, of course, they normally had no opportunity to spend more than a few hours together at any one time.

How on earth would they cope, thought David, *if Will did come back?* He knew it was Hetty who would suffer most if this did happen.

He had told his mother that he saw his job as one of loving and caring for Hetty whatever happened—and he had meant it. He had told Hetty that they would work things out together whatever happened, and he meant it.

Somehow because the future was so unpredictable, he had to make these months count. He had to give her positive, loving, inspiring memories that she could look back on and treasure, whatever happened.

One evening as they sat together listening to the wireless, just before Janet was due to return, Fred Astaire's voice came through the airwaves.

Someday, when I'm awfully low, When the world is cold, I will feel aglow Just thinking of you, And the way you look tonight.

David put his arm around Hetty, turning her to face him on the settee where they were sitting.

"That's what I feel about you. Every time you hear that song, please remember that's what I feel about you.

"And what's more, it's the way I will always think about you, no matter what happens," he added tenderly.

The tears started to Hetty's eyes, which nevertheless were shining.

"It's the way I feel about you too."

"Yes, but I want you to remember how much I love you and how lovely I think you are every time you hear that song. Will you promise me you'll do that?"

"You're being very demanding this evening."

But David wouldn't be distracted or take his eyes off her and was obviously still waiting for an answer.

"Yes, all right, I promise."

And, of course, that necessitated a kiss.

---ooo000ooo---

Hetty looked back on the time when Peggy with Sarah and Peter stayed with them in Wells as one of the happiest times of her life.

After a few sharp words at the beginning of her stay, which modified a little after she had met David, Peggy accepted the situation she found herself in and did her best to make the last few weeks before Hetty's baby was due as comfortable as possible for her.

Janet and Peggy soon became firm friends and Mary blossomed with the attention she received from her cousins.

"You mustn't worry too much about Mum and Dad," Peggy tried to reassure Hetty.

"I know they were very upset when they got your letter, but they will come around. It was Dad who gave me the train fare to come down here. They love you very much."

"I'm so glad. I wished so much that I'd had you to talk to. Somehow you always used to make things better for me when we were little."

Peggy laughed.

"And you always used to make things worse for me. But I am glad we were able to come.

"And have you noticed how much Peter is enjoying David's company? He misses his father so much. I'm grateful to David for taking notice of him the way he does. It's such a help."

"He's a schoolteacher that's why."

"No, it's more than that. He takes trouble with him. You're a very lucky girl."

---ooo000ooo---

When the time came, the baby arrived with the minimum of fuss.

David was so delighted that it was a little girl.

"I wanted a girl so much because I hoped she'd be like you."

Hetty laughed as she looked at the baby's little screwed up face.

"Well, she doesn't look like me. At least I hope not.

"I think she's got your eyes though," she added thoughtfully.

They called the baby Dorothy.

Mary was busily playing with her cousins and Margaret from along the road and so hardly noticed the new arrival for the time being.

---ooo000ooo---

Peggy wanted to return home just before Christmas and a day before she was due to go, Janet invited them all, including Penny and her children, for an informal goodbye party.

Rationing didn't allow more than a few sandwiches and some jelly for the children, but it was nevertheless a very happy occasion.

To finish the evening, Peggy, who was a good pianist, sat at the piano, and Peter was given a cymbal, Sarah some maracas and Mary a wooden spoon with a saucepan lid to strike, while they sang carols and popular songs together. Flicking through the book, Hetty suddenly came across 'their' song.

"Play this, play this for me, Peggy. I want to sing this."

She had a tuneful mellow lilting voice and she sang it well, her eyes fixed on David, meaningfully, as she began.

However, he almost immediately butted in with a joke, saying that the song was no good for the children and their instruments, so it came to an abrupt end before it had really started.

She was disappointed, especially as David found the music for the wartime song, 'Pack up your Troubles' and got them all playing their instruments and singing together again instead.

She found out the reason for this as she walked with him to the bus stop later in the evening. He'd had too much to carry to cycle that evening.

"Why didn't you let me sing our song? Why did you change the music?"

"I thought you'd probably forgotten that Janet has only recently lost her husband and that Peggy and Penny are both missing theirs badly, so I thought it would be better to make them laugh instead."

"Our love is something that we express privately to each other. You're a kind person, so I'm sure that if you'd had time to think you wouldn't have done that."

Hetty's heart sank and she felt terrible about it, especially as she quickly realised, he was right. And as David's bus arrived at that moment, with a quick peck on her cheek he had gone before they had time to talk about it.

---ooo000ooo---

The evening was spoiled and although Hetty put on a brave face for the others when she returned to the house, she was hurting so badly inside she just wanted to be alone.

She lay awake for many hours that night, first feeling angry with David for what he had said and the way he had rejected her, and then feeling angry with herself as she gradually realised that he was right.

Thinking back, she had noticed her sister's face, but she'd been too intent on singing her song to realise what she was doing.

How thoughtless of her. And then she began to wonder what the other women would have thought of her and her misery was complete.

Peggy noticed something was wrong at breakfast the next morning.

"You look a bit miserable. There's nothing wrong, is there?"

"No, no. I've just realised how much I'm going to miss you, that's all."

"I'll come and see you again, don't worry."

Peggy was practical.

"I think it should be easier for you to get out and about now that the baby has arrived. You could be looking after someone else's baby. Plenty of people do it."

"Peggy, you've been so good to me."

"I'm so sorry it is so difficult for you with Tom away, but I can't tell you what a difference it's made that you were able to come to be with me. Thank you so very much."

Hetty forced herself to speak cheerfully. She couldn't spoil their last morning together.

---ooo000ooo---

Peggy, Sarah and Peter caught the 12.40 train to London, and having waved them off, Hetty spent a miserable afternoon sorting the bedrooms out and generally getting everything back to normal ready for Janet's return from work.

Mary was more demanding than usual, having lost the company of her cousins, and Dorothy also seemed to sense her misery and was unusually fretful.

Hetty didn't even know whether David would be coming over for the evening.

They usually arranged when they would see each other next from day to day, but there hadn't been an opportunity to do so yesterday.

However, David arrived a little earlier than usual and Janet opened the door.

"She's just reading Mary her story.

"She's looking a bit peaky and low today, but I suppose that's because Peggy and the children have gone."

"Incidentally, Penny's asked me to babysit for her this evening—in case you were thinking of going out for a walk."

David took the stairs two at a time. He put his head round the door.

"Can I help?" he asked.

Hetty had Mary sitting on her lap and the baby, Dorothy, on her arm as she was trying to read Mary her story and rock Dorothy at the same time.

She nodded briefly and was glad to hand Dorothy to David to rock instead.

"I'm sorry the bus had to arrive just as we were talking yesterday. I could see you needed a good hug."

Hetty nodded sadly. "I don't know how I could have been so thoughtless."

"I want my story," whined Mary. "Why've you stopped Mummy? I want my story."

As often with babies, the change of arms had done the trick and David was soon looking down wonderingly at his sleeping baby.

Later that evening while Janet was out babysitting for Penny, they at last had time to talk and feel comfortable in each other's love again.

"I'm too impulsive, that's my problem. It's always been one of my biggest faults."

Now it was David's turn to sigh.

"The trouble is that I love your impulsiveness, so I suppose I can't have it both ways. It was just that I was worried about the others."

"You were right. And the children were having such fun. It would have been a shame to stop that."

"Our love for each other needs to include everyone when we are in company and only become private and personal when we are alone together…like now!

"I do still want it to be 'our' song and I do want our memories of it to be happy ones."

And so, they sang their song softly to each other as Mary and Dorothy dropped off to sleep.

Someday, when I'm awfully low…

It became the prelude to an evening of more than usually tender loving, secure in the knowledge that Janet was babysitting elsewhere.

---ooo000ooo---

Part Two

The second telegram was brief and to the point like the first.

Second Lieutenant Will Thomas, formerly reported as missing, presumed dead, has been found to be alive and in a Japanese Prisoners of War Camp.

The words swam in front of Hetty's eyes.
Will had been missing for over two years.
Dorothy was three months old.
She stared at the postboy incomprehensibly.

"Are you sure this is for me?" she asked as he handed the telegram to her.

"If that's your name it must be for you. Is it bad news? Do you want me to call someone?"

"No, it's not bad news. It's just such a shock."

The post boy nodded. He was getting used to scenes like this.

"Well, if you're sure you're all right, I'll be going."

---ooo000ooo---

Hetty sat at the kitchen table staring at nothing, her thoughts in complete turmoil.

Will was alive! She ought to be glad. She was glad in a way. She had worried so much, she had imagined so many terrors. It was wonderful news. Mavis and Arnold would be thrilled. Mary would have a father again.

David would be... David, David, David! What would David's reaction be?

He was generous and loving. He would be delighted.

But did she want him to be delighted?

What would that mean for her relationship with him?

She loved David.

She had somehow felt as if Will's absence had gone on for so long that it would go on for ever and that in the fullness of time, she and David would be able to get married.

She knew that David thought the same way.

And I want to marry him, thought Hetty. *I want to marry him. But Will, poor Will.*

She made herself think back to their brief time together.

There had been a lot of fun.

She thought of their early days at the church youth club.

Will had been the life and soul of that club.

She had been pleased to be his girlfriend.

She wondered what had happened to him.

Would he be the same?

Mavis and Arnold would be thrilled.

Mavis and Arnold...goodness, she must tell them the good news.

Janet wouldn't mind her borrowing her telephone just once in these circumstances. They needed to know straightaway.

She knew what she would have felt like if Mary had been lost and found.

Mavis answered the phone tentatively, sounding surprised that someone was ringing in the middle of the day.

"Mavis, it's Hetty here."

"Hetty, my goodness, is everything all right?"

"It certainly is. I've just had a telegram and they've found Will!"

There was a gasp at the other end and then silence.

"Mavis, Mavis are you all right?"

"Yes, yes. I just had to sit down, that's all. Tell me what's happened."

"I'll read you the telegram.

"Second Lieutenant Will Thomas, formerly reported as missing, presumed dead, has been found to be alive and in a Japanese Prisoner of War Camp."

"That's wonderful. Wonderful news. I hope he's really all right though; I don't trust those people. There have been a few horrible stories filtering through."

"I know. I worry about that too."

"Never mind, at least he's alive. I must go and tell Arnold straight away. Is it all right if I come across tomorrow, as usual, to see Mary?"

"Yes, of course. I shall look forward to seeing you."

She put the phone down and went and sat down at the table again and just stared out of the window. She couldn't think what she ought to be doing, so she just sat there. She felt devoid of all feeling.

A cry from Dorothy roused her and somehow, she got through the rest of the day.

Janet was alarmed by her pallor when she arrived home from work.

"What on earth is the matter? You look like death warmed up!"

"I had a telegram this morning. Will is alive. He's in a Japanese Prisoner of War Camp."

"Oh, you poor dear, what a shock you've had. No wonder you're pale."

She was wise enough not to make further comment but concentrated instead on getting some food into Hetty and helping her with the children.

She said nothing when David arrived—except to comment that she was going out to see a friend in a minute or two and wouldn't be in until late.

Hetty didn't look at him as he walked through the door knowing that she would start crying if she did.

Instead she just pointed to the telegram on the dressing table.

She was as usual reading Mary's bedtime story, while Dorothy was already fast asleep in her cot.

David read the telegram and went as white as a sheet himself.

He sat down heavily on the bottom of Mary's bed and put his head in his hands.

Hetty finished the story, tucked up Mary and they went downstairs.

He pulled her to him when they reached the sitting room. She noticed the tears in his eyes and on his cheeks and that at last released the floodgates of her own.

He pulled her onto his lap and they sat and wept together.

"We always knew this might happen."

"But we never believed it would. I feel so awful because I should be rejoicing because he's alive and instead I'm crying."

"It's partly the shock. After all you've believed him dead for well over two years now—and then to be told he's alive and in a prisoner of war camp! It's unbelievable!"

Then he remembered his encounter with Mavis, when she made sure he knew that she thought Will was alive.

"Have you told Mavis and Arnold?" He was anxious.

"Yes, I telephoned them and spoke to Mavis. She got an awful shock too, but she's thrilled, of course. She's coming over tomorrow to see Mary, as usual."

David sighed.

"We should be thrilled too, and I am in a way. We thought he was dead and he's alive. It's wonderful news really. It's just us…" he tailed off lamely.

"I know. All the plans we had for after the war—together."

Hetty's sobs broke out again.

"There is such a thing as divorce, we could still be together, couldn't we, couldn't we?"

"Of course, there is, but Hetty, when Dorothy was born, I checked on our legal position with a solicitor.

"If you asked Will to divorce you because of your relationship with me and the birth of Dorothy, he could refuse to divorce you and in addition refuse to have Dorothy as part of his household.

"If he did agree to divorce you, you would lose Mary as she would have to go to him unless he agreed otherwise."

"Surely not! Surely nobody could take Mary—or Dorothy—from me? They're my children!"

"I'm afraid the law's not on our side in this. That's what would happen and my solicitor friend said that there wouldn't be any point in fighting it as we would lose."

Hetty was aghast and silent while fear and nameless horrors clutched at her heart.

"But Will's not a monster. By all accounts, he's a nice chap and you must have loved him once or you would never have married him."

"Being in a Japanese Prisoner of War Camp must be terrible. And we don't know what he went through before he got there."

"Could we really let him come back to the sort of mess we are suggesting?"

"Could we really let him come home to a wife who's left him after all he must have been through?"

"Could you do that to him? Could I do that to him?"

"I suppose not."

Hetty was first of all miserable for herself and then began to realise the impact Will's return would have on David.

"But what about you?"

"How can I leave you?"

"I love you, I love you, I love you! I can't leave you! I won't leave you!"

His reply was swift.

"I love you too and I feel that I can't leave you and won't leave you."

"But then I think of Mary. If you have me, then you will probably lose her.

"I love Mary and I don't like to think of what it would do to her to lose her mother.

"And anyway, I know in my heart that you would never dream of leaving her.

"You're not that sort of woman, not that sort of mother. You would eventually resent it terribly and finally you would turn against me as a result."

Hetty was silent once more and then spoke more thoughtfully.

"I can't imagine ever turning against you, but nor can I imagine losing Mary, either."

"Oh why, oh why did it all have to turn out like this!"

"We shall just have to make the best of a bad job."

"Of course, we can't help asking why this has happened, but it's a fruitless question to ask because there's no answer, so it's no good tormenting ourselves by trying to find it."

"Instead we have to be practical and positive and plan to make the best of a bad job."

Hetty almost hit him, she was so furious, as she leapt off his lap.

"How can you say things like that?"

"How can you be so reasonable and sit there making plans. Of course, we must ask why, why, why?"

"I thought you loved me! I see now that it doesn't go very deep!"

"You haven't even begun to think of a real way out! You promised you'd never leave me, remember?"

"I thought that somehow we were going to work things out together! Instead you're just pussyfooting around!"

"I expect you're glad that I shall have to go back to Will and that you'll be rid of me!"

"I expect you can't wait! Well you'd better go! I can't bear to have you around anymore! Go on, leave me! Get out! Get out! Get out now!" she screamed.

David shook her hard and pushed her down into a chair, standing over her so that she couldn't get out and glared at her.

"No, I will not get out! How dare you speak to me like that!"

"How dare you suggest that I don't love you when you know damn well, I do!"

"The trouble with you is that you're selfish and you've somehow always managed to get your own way and whatever you want."

"Well now you've got to think of other people for a change and it's high time you did."

"Think about Will and all he's been through!"

"Think of Mavis and Arnold and how thrilled they will be to see him!"

"Think of your children! They need you!"

"I won't ask you to think of me because it will only infuriate you further but sometime when you're calmer, you should do so."

"You won't be the only loser in all of this you know. I will lose everything too."

His voice was breaking now.

"I'd better go… There's no point in my staying any longer.

"But don't you dare think I'm abandoning you, because I'm not and nor will I ever abandon you."

Hetty's anger was at last subsiding.

"I'm sorry. I didn't mean any of that. I'm sorry."

"Are you?" David's voice was cold.

"It was there underneath or it wouldn't have come out."

"It's just that I'm so frightened. I'm so very frightened. And I just don't know what to do."

She was sobbing.

David hesitated for a moment and then pulled her up into his arms again and hushed her head against his shoulder, where it remained as they comforted each other.

In spite of this, they, neither of them, slept that night.

---ooo000ooo---

What Hetty hadn't realised, thought David later, *was that she would probably lose Dorothy.* If Will was anything like his father, David couldn't think that he would want the child.

Neither do I want him to have her, he thought grimly.

"Hetty is a good and loving mother, but if Will resents Dorothy and shows it, it will do her untold damage."

But if Will wouldn't have Dorothy, then he would have to look after her himself and how on earth could he look after a baby and earn enough to keep them both as well?

"I suppose I'd have to take in private, paying pupils. I'd hate that, but I can't see any other way out."

Maureen was quite worried about his pallor at breakfast the next morning.

"Are you all right? You're not brewing anything, are you?"

David told her what had happened.

"Poor Hetty, she hasn't really taken in yet that if Will won't accept Dorothy, then she will have to leave her with me. She has no choice.

"Either she stays with Will and keeps Mary, or she leaves Will and comes to me with Dorothy and probably has to leave Mary behind—unless Will is very understanding."

Maureen saw the problem straight away.

"She can't do that to Mary and knowing Hetty, I'm sure she won't.

"Will would have to find a complete stranger to look after her. You can't just abandon a child to that. And Mary doesn't even remember Will."

"I know," David sighed.

"But if Will won't accept Dorothy, what on earth will you do?"

"I've been thinking about that all night.

"I think I'll have to take in private pupils to tutor and manage somehow that way. I'll have to move to Wells where there are more people.

"I imagine I could take over Hetty's rooms as Janet is always very friendly.

"Then there would be Penny up the road to help as well in emergencies."

"I'll help too." Maureen was thoughtful.

"In fact," she added slowly, "I suppose I could sell up here and we could buy a small house in Wells, preferably in that area where they live, and manage that way."

David gave his mother a hug.

"You're very kind, as usual, Mother. But I couldn't ask you to do that. I'll manage somehow on my own."

"I'll move to Wells anyway, whatever you say. So you can either live with me or with Janet—it's up to you!"

---ooo000ooo---

It was Mavis and Arnold who made Hetty realise what would happen to Dorothy.

Arnold did not usually accompany Mavis on her visits to see Mary, but this was a special occasion and Hetty was touched by the joy on their faces when they arrived early afternoon.

She showed them the telegram straight away.

"Well, Mary, isn't that exciting news! Your daddy is all right and one of these days you are going to see him again! Aren't you pleased?"

"Yes," Mary sounded a bit doubtful as she was not really sure what they were talking about. She couldn't remember her father at all.

"And Dorothy will be pleased too," she added.

"Well…"

Mavis hesitated but there was no hesitation about Arnold's words. He now knew all about the baby and definitely did not approve.

"I don't think so. I think it will just be you and Mummy going back to meet Daddy," he added meaningfully.

"Oh, why's that, Mummy?"

"We don't know what will happen yet. We'll just have to wait and see, won't we?"

She forced herself to smile.

"But we're all looking forward to seeing Daddy whatever happens."

Mavis and Arnold left to take Mary out to tea.

---ooo000ooo---

"It's such a lovely evening," said Janet later, when David arrived.

"Why don't you take Hetty for a walk once the children have dropped off? I'll babysit for you."

"I don't know what we'd do without people like you. You've been so very kind."

"It's no hardship being kind to nice people. And you and Hetty have been good to me too, you know. I was finding it so difficult to cope with the death of Ernie and having Hetty staying here and you popping in all the time has made all the difference to me."

David smiled and was silent.

"I'm so sorry you've got so many hard decisions to make. Don't forget that if there's anything I can do to help; I'll be only too pleased."

David gave her a warm smile as he climbed the stairs to find Hetty.

"Thank you, I know that."

---ooo000ooo---

Hetty put her fingers to her lips as he entered. Mary was just dropping off and Dorothy was already fast asleep in her cot.

It was a perfect April evening and they started their walk through the cathedral grounds, enjoying the blossom and the profusion of spring flowers in spite of their sadness.

They were silent for a long time, both anxious to avoid the pain of further acrimonious discussion, and somehow staying silent prolonged the illusion that all was well.

Finally, it was Hetty who spoke.

"Mavis and Arnold came this afternoon..." her voice trailed off as a sob escaped.

David turned to face her, catching hold of both her hands.

"And?" he asked, gently.

"Mary, in her innocence, asked them if Dorothy would be coming back with us to Daddy."

"Oh dear. What was their reaction?"

"Arnold said, 'I don't think so'…

"Oh David, what are we to do?"

He was urgent in his reply.

"Hetty, you do know how much I love you, don't you?"

"Yes, yes, of course I do and I love you too—but what's that got to do with it?"

"Would you trust me to look after Dorothy?" he asked tentatively.

"Of course, I'd trust you with Dorothy any time. You're her father, after all."

David then tried to explain what he'd been thinking.

"I didn't mean any time Hetty, I meant for all time. I love her. I'm her father."

"To have her would mean that I had a little bit of you to hold on to and to cherish."

"Do you remember how Janet told you that above all else when Ernie died, she wished that she had had his child?"

"Well, if you're going to have to go away, Hetty, leave me our child."

He lifted her fingers to his lips and kissed them one by one, making them wet with the tears which were now rolling quietly down his cheeks.

"I suppose I've got no choice," said Hetty brokenly.

"Yes, Hetty. You have got a choice. You could leave Will and come to me, hoping that he would let you bring Mary."

"I would do that like a shot if he would let me have Mary, you know that. But would he let me have her? Can I take that risk with her?"

"Hetty, you haven't answered my question. Would you let me have Dorothy?

"If we are going to make any sense of this mess, we've got to let our love take the initiative and make our plans together regardless of what Will may or may not do.

"Now, for the third time, would you let me have Dorothy?" His voice was soft and gentle.

Hetty searched his eyes for a long time as he looked steadily back at her. Finally, she managed a small tremulous smile.

"You're the most wonderful man in the world, David. I trust you with my love, I would trust you with my life, and of course I trust you with our child."

She resisted the temptation to lay her head on David's shoulder and weep. She couldn't bear to hurt him again.

---ooo000ooo---

Two weeks later Hetty had a letter from Will.

Dear Hetty,

I cannot believe that the Red Cross have finally discovered us in this hellhole and that news will have got out that we are still alive. Only just alive, I'm afraid! They've treated us like animals—and worse. Quite a few have died, one way or another. But perhaps things will improve now that we've been officially registered.

It's only been the thought of you that has kept me alive, Hetty. I think of you all the time and of our little daughter, Mary, and try to imagine what you're doing and how you are. In the worst of times if I have managed to concentrate on you, I've somehow managed to put up with everything else.

Will you write to me now, Hetty? Please write soon and send photographs of you and Mary. The photo I carried with me was lost when we were captured, so I can't show off to the others how beautiful you are and what a sweet little daughter we've got! I'm so proud of you both.

I miss you so much Hetty and long for the time when we shall be together again and living like a proper family. I make lots of plans all the while for that time, I can tell you. We all do. It is the only thing that keeps us sane when everything around us seems hopeless.

Write soon, my dearest.

Your ever-loving husband,
Will

Hetty smiled a little to herself as she finished reading. Somehow, she could almost hear Will talking. And she remembered he always had been proud of her.

She'd never really had a love letter from Will before. He'd never been much good at telling her that he loved her—not like David.

But it's not fair to compare them, she thought. *And anyway, there is no comparison. Will was her sweetheart. David was her love.*

How could she ever manage to go back to Will and pretend that everything was the same? How on earth could she do it?

The letter did show her one thing very clearly, though. She had to go back to him.

The thought of her had obviously kept him going through some very bad times. He needed her. He needed her badly.

She had loved him once and she still loved him in a way and certainly cared about his well-being.

If David had taught her nothing else, he had taught her that real love was giving love whether or not there was any return.

She was somehow going to have to give love to Will because he was going to need it.

She would talk to David about it, perhaps he would help her.

---ooo000ooo---

David was silent for a long time after reading the letter. There was no real word of love in it for Hetty.

No thought for the pain she must have gone through.

Will was proud of his possession of her and Mary. That's what came through most strongly.

David feared for her. The desolate look in Hetty's eyes when she spoke about him that night in the cinema flashed back into his mind. Oh dear!

"How does the letter make you feel?"

Hetty was thoughtful.

"I suppose it has made me realise that I can't just abandon him. He has obviously been through a terrible time and he needs me."

"I've thought a lot about what you said in your anger about me being selfish, you know, and I've realised you were right. I have been very selfish about everything—including you.

"And I don't think I can go on being like that and retain any sort of self-respect."

"Trust me to say something that has made you decide to go back to him."

David teased her ruefully, his heart sinking.

"I'm just as bad, you know. I want you for myself and myself alone, but when I think about it, I know that I'm just being selfish too."

"And we can't just deny our love and smother it because Will is coming home. It won't go away."

"Somehow, we have to use it to give love, not only to each other, but to Dorothy and Mary and yes," he sighed, "to Will.

"I still remember what you said to me on that epic walk, you see. Do you remember?"

Hetty smiled.

"No. What on earth was it?"

"You said, '*What you forget in your grief is that you still need to give love as well as receive it.*'

"I thought that was inspired at the time and I still do. It has certainly helped me these last few days. Think about it yourself again, Hetty."

"Yes, I do remember that now. My friends at church helped me find that out and it did help."

"You were experiencing the pain of separation then, and of possible bereavement."

"What we shall experience when Will returns will be much the same."

"Both of us have already experienced that real love is painful and we shall hurt and hurt a lot."

"The time we've had together has been wonderful, but we're going to have to pay a very high price for it."

"I know, but I wouldn't have been without our time together for anything."

"And to try to think of never having told each other that we loved each other is just impossible."

"Well then. We've got to make the most of that love one way or another!"

"I'm sorry I made you so angry with my talk of plans the other day and I understand why."

"But I can't and won't deny my love for you and that this brief eighteen months we've had together has been the happiest time of my life. We can't just push that under the carpet."

"How do you mean?"

"Well, we've already begun to make a loving plan for Dorothy's future and must talk more about that to sort out how to make it work."

"But in the meantime, we've got to make loving plans together for your future and my future and Mary's, of course."

"I don't see how we possibly can."

Hetty was rather exasperated.

"We don't know what's going to happen."

"But whatever happens we can still feed our love."

"I don't see how. I don't see how we can even write to each other. I don't imagine Will would like that."

"I didn't mean just writing to each other, although we could do that via your sister, Peggy, if she wouldn't mind."

"But even if we can't do that we already have 'our' song. Every time we hear that, we think of each other. But, apart from that, I know another way of being together in our thoughts—though it probably involves a walk down the garden…"

Hetty laughed. "Whatever do you mean?"

"My Mother has a tree in her garden, a crab apple, that she gave my father on his 50th birthday, when it was blossoming. I remember that we danced around it as we sang Happy Birthday to him! Since he died, I see her standing under it sometimes and I know she's talking to him."

"Then in the spring, when it's flowering, she is so delighted as its petals become luminous in the sunshine for a short time around his birthday and the joy of them reaches into her kitchen from the garden."

"In autumn, around the time he died, there is blossom in his tree again as she has grown a vibrant violet clematis up it. Although it is the colour of mourning, there is always hope in it as the sun transforms it to a royal shade as it reaches higher and higher in the tree."

"Oh, and she makes jelly from the crab apples too and we enjoy that throughout the year."

"Let's each plant a tree, or even a bush, which we'll buy for each other, and plant in our gardens in the same way. What about it? What do you think it should be?"

"Yes, that sounds a good idea. I like the thought of that and that it's always there. Perhaps we could each plant a crab apple too…?"

"We could also even have a time each day when we think of each other," she added smiling

David smiled too.

"I'd like that. How about lunchtime? Apart from Saturday and Sunday, Will will normally be at work at lunchtime."

"We could turn on the radio in time for the weather forecast before the news, and as we hear whether it's going to rain or not in Somerset or London, we could think of each other!"

Hetty laughed and David gave her a hug.

"That's the first time I've heard you laugh for weeks."

"Do you remember telling me I was beautiful when I laughed? That meant a lot to me."

"Yes, of course I do. And you've remembered it. So that just makes my point about all these other things, doesn't it!"

And they laughed together and felt comforted.

Maureen had been true to her word and their cottage in the village had sold quickly. Meantime she had found a small house not far from Janet or from Penny and her children and moved into it.

David and Hetty had decided that the best way for him to learn how to look after Dorothy was to ask if he could stay in Janet's spare room during the Easter Holidays and this was working well.

An added bonus, of course, was that they saw much more of each other, though this was also painful as they realised how good it felt and how short a time they had together.

David had given his notice in for the end of the summer term and was looking around to see what tutoring and other work he could find in Wells.

As the summer holiday approached, Hetty and David decided that the next stage in preparing themselves and Dorothy and Mary for the time when Will returned, would be for Hetty and Mary to go to stay with Peggy for a time, leaving David in full charge of Dorothy.

He would move back in with his mother with her while Hetty and Mary were away.

"But why can't Dorothy come with us too?" asked Mary.

So Hetty explained.

"David needs Dorothy to keep him company while we go to stay with Aunty Peggy and Sarah and Peter."

---ooo000ooo---

Now that it was known that Will was still alive, Hetty was receiving Will's salary, rather than a meagre widow's pension.

She also realised, while she was staying with Peggy, that she would also need to find somewhere for them to live when Will came home.

Nobody had any idea when that would be, but she had to be prepared and the summer holiday was an ideal time to start—and to find a new school for Mary.

David kissed her goodbye.

"Let's start practising remembering each other by all our special things. Then we can see how it will work. And don't expect it to be easy, because it won't be."

"And be a good girl, Mary." He lifted her up and swung her round.

"And give my love to Sarah and Peter, won't you—and Aunty Peggy, of course."

---ooo000ooo---

The holiday with Peggy and the children was not an unqualified success. Hetty missed both David and Dorothy terribly and found it hard not to be irritable as a result.

Peggy finally got rather fed up and tackled her.

"Look here, Hetty. You'll have to stop moaning because I can't bear it anymore. There are a lot of people far worse off than you, you know."

"At least all the people you love are still alive. You just can't live your life wishing for things to be different from the way they are. You'll go mad if you do."

Hetty felt terrible. She wasn't managing very well. What Peggy had said was just the sort of thing that David might have said. She must try harder.

That evening as they sat listening to the radio, Fred Astaire's voice came floating over it singing 'their' song.

"There is nothing for me but to love you…just the way you look tonight."

She smiled and thought of David and then found relief as her tears flowed, and from that moment onwards things began to go better.

---ooo000ooo---

She found a small house in Harrow, about half an hour's bus-ride from where Peggy lived in Hounslow, and only about fifteen minutes' walk from her parents, so it seemed ideal.

Mary was very excited at the thought of having her own bedroom, and Hetty began to enjoy getting the house furnished—mainly with hand-me-downs from her parents and Peggy, but also from adverts in the local paper. Finding curtains was more difficult as they required coupons that were urgently needed for clothes, but by dint of help from friends and family and her own ability to sew, she soon had everything looking very nice.

The trouble is, she thought, *I'm really enjoying getting this ready for David and me…and it won't be David and me, it will be Will.*

The plan now was to return to Wells for the rest of the summer holiday before moving into the Harrow house just before the start of the autumn term, so that Mary could get settled into her new school.

David and Dorothy were delighted to see them, and so was Janet.

Hetty and Mary moved back in with Janet and David and Dorothy seemed happily settled in Maureen's new house.

Hetty knew she ought to be pleased that Dorothy had settled and was responding so well to Maureen, but she found it very hard that 'her' baby no longer seemed to be hers.

David read the look in her eye and tried to help her to come to terms with it and Maureen was tactful, but she still found it a very painful two weeks.

Mary, on the other hand, seemed to accept how things had changed quite happily and was full of talk of her cousins and her new bedroom back in Harrow.

Hetty had, of course, written to Will and sent him the photographs he requested, which had been taken specially by a Wells photographer, and a second letter came from him while she was down there.

Dear Hetty,

Your letter and photos arrived safely and I've already shown them proudly around the camp. What a little beauty our daughter is and I love the way you are doing your hair these days. You look so glamorous.

Things haven't changed much here at the moment, though the regime is slightly less rigorous and brutal than it was.

I'm living just for the time when we're reunited—in the full sense.

Your ever-loving husband,
Will.

Hetty was pleased the photos had gone down well. It had been David's idea to have them taken professionally. He had one that she hadn't sent to Will and it was already sitting on the sideboard in Maureen's house.

"Have you found some work yet?" was one of Hetty's first questions to him, anxious as to how they would manage otherwise, especially as Maureen had given up her job to move to Wells.

"I'm going to be teaching mornings only at the local grammar school, while Mother looks after Dorothy.

"Then in the afternoons and evenings, I'll take over as I don't want her to get too tired.

"I've also taken on one or two pupils for individual coaching in the evening when Dorothy is in bed. So, one way or another, we should be all right."

Hetty was relieved. It had worked out far better than she had feared.

"How did you make out with our remembering plans?"

"Not very well, really," Hetty was truthful.

"I nearly drove Peggy mad for a time. Then one evening I heard Fred Astaire singing our song, and from then on it got better."

"I was much the same. But the first bit is bound to be the worst. It will get easier, I'm sure."

Hetty wished that she had his confidence.

---ooo000ooo---

Their last evening together came all too quickly. Maureen was babysitting for Dorothy and Janet for Mary.

They had wondered about affording a last meal together at a local hotel but decided instead to buy fish and chips and have one last long walk together to keep up the tradition they had established.

It was also blackberrying time again, so they would have a readymade dessert as they walked, while Janet and Maureen would be glad of any they could bring home.

Both had determined to hold back their emotions somehow so as not to waste the last few hours of heart to heart talking that they longed for above all else.

Of course, they could have spent a last night together in a hotel, but that no longer seemed appropriate since the arrival of Will's letters.

They really needed a lifetime of physical loving and a night-time, though tempting, would just be too frustrating to bear.

The adaptation to their new forms of loving was already cutting in and they needed to build the basis for that above all else.

Then an urgent request came from Hetty.

"But I will need letters from you. I don't think I can manage at all without letters and I asked Peggy if she would mind you writing to me there, and she doesn't."

"It means that I can only catch up with them when I can get across to see her, but I'll need that lifeline, I'll really need that point of contact with you if I'm going to be able to cope, and I'll need to know how Dorothy is too, of course."

David responded in the same vein.

"I'll need letters too. It was so difficult after you'd left to stay with Peggy. I kept thinking of so much that I wanted to talk to you about…and you weren't there! It was terrible."

Hetty felt an echo of her longing and loneliness while she was staying with Peggy in his words.

"I suppose perhaps your letters to me had better normally be written at Peggy's house as well, unless you find that you can write and post them while Will is at work."

"I know. And what makes me feel terrible is the thought of leaving your letters to me at Peggy's as well. I couldn't bear Will to find them—and anyway it wouldn't be fair on him. But it will be dreadful not to be able to read them whenever I want to."

Hetty sounded tearful

"Do you think we are being very unfair to him to think of keeping in touch in this way at all? It's just that I don't think I can manage otherwise."

He took her hand in his to comfort her and tried to keep the pessimism out of his voice.

"We don't really know what Will will be like when he returns. It probably isn't fair—but we've had to compromise and give up so much anyway, I really don't think we need to feel guilty about this."

"It's just letters we're talking about. It's not as if we are going to try and have a secret meeting every few weeks."

"I wouldn't mind a few of those as well as letters!" the words burst out of her.

"I know," David was thoughtful. "If only we could meet! I've thought about it quite a lot and wondered whether there was any way we could manage it."

"You'll want to see Dorothy occasionally—and me as well I hope—but we'll have to wait and see how it can be worked out if at all.

"Perhaps I could bring Dorothy up to stay with Peggy sometimes—but that would be difficult if the other children talk about it in Will's presence.

"We'll have to play it by ear when the time comes."

And so, they made plans.

But before the evening was out their talk turned to love and Hetty was silenced as David poured out his heart to her, talking about every moment of their time together it seemed.

He told her how much it had meant to him and how he had loved her at every stage of it. He hardly stopped for breath.

Finally, she forced a few words into his monologue reiterating her love for him.

"Above all else, you've made me feel that you value me, and that somehow I am worthy of your love—although my heart tells me that I'm not."

"Don't you dare ever say that or even think it," his voice cracked.

"I shall feel a complete failure if you say that and it will be as if all my loving has been in vain.

"I would like to have had a lifetime of telling you how much I love you and instead have had only these few months, so that I've often felt as if my heart would burst with so much to tell you in words—and deeds—in so little time."

Hetty's tears threatened in spite of her efforts.

She struggled hard with them and then said trying to tease and smiling a little, "Well you'll just have to write it all down instead, then, won't you!

"You'll have to spend your time writing me wonderful love letters! I can't wait."

"I'll need to hear from you too. I'll need it so badly. I get so worried that somehow you won't be able to write when Will returns, won't be able to get across to Peggy's house."

"I'll find a way. I promise you; I'll find a way…"

---ooo000ooo---

Part Three

Mary was delighted with her daddy when she came out of school, especially as he lifted her high on his shoulder to carry her home.

Peggy was telephoned as were Hetty's parents and soon they all arrived and there was a noisy welcome home party going on with all the neighbours taking part as well.

Tom, Peggy's husband still wasn't home, but plenty of other husbands were and Will soon found himself telling the story of his capture and imprisonment over and over again.

Hetty remembered Mavis and Arnold too.

"You must telephone your parents. Ring them now. They were going to come on Thursday to stay for a few days, but they could come tomorrow if you'd rather."

"I'd rather have you to myself. Let's leave the arrangement as you made it and let them come on Thursday after we've had two days together."

Hetty was relieved. She wanted time to get to know Will again before his parents arrived.

And she also wanted time to tell him about David and Dorothy herself.

Although she trusted Mavis, she didn't trust Arnold and was afraid he might betray her in some unfortunate way.

She and David had decided that it was better to be matter of fact and truthful about what had happened in the hope that Will would accept it as another of the casualties of war.

However, it didn't work out like that and no matter how hard Hetty tried to find an opportune moment to talk to Will, it didn't come.

And he didn't—wouldn't—tell her about what had happened to him or to his back.

"I want to forget it," he was brusque.

"I don't want to talk about it, so don't ask!"

But on the same grounds, he never once asked her how she had got on and what had happened to her. He didn't seem to want to know.

Instead intercourse and more intercourse was at the top of his agenda. Sometimes Hetty felt as if he was using her body to try to forget all that had happened to his.

Perhaps it's the only way he can forget, she *thought.* Whatever the cause, she found it extremely difficult as it was brief and demanding with no tenderness. And where was the love?

What you forget in your grief is that you still need to give love as well as receive it.

Hetty hung on to her conversations with David, and she tried so hard to give herself and to go on giving herself, but it seemed as if the more she gave the more Will demanded until she almost felt as if he was gradually eating her up.

It was almost as if she herself didn't count any more, as if she wasn't giving her body anymore but it was being taken whether she wanted it or not.

There was no glimmer of pleasure or joy in it for her. It was simply a continuing conquest while she bravely tried and tried to go on giving and giving again.

The tears would come quietly late at night when Will was asleep and she would try to calm herself with thoughts of David looking at her, loving her, singing with her…

Someday, when I'm awfully low, When the world is cold, I will feel aglow, Just thinking of you, And the way you look tonight.

Mavis and Arnold's visit came and went without incident to Hetty's great relief. She had managed to get Mavis on one side as she arrived and whispered to her quickly.

"I haven't had an opportunity to tell him about Dorothy yet.

"He's been badly hurt in the Concentration Camp, Mavis. He's been beaten. There are weals all down his back," and the tears stood in Hetty's eyes as she spoke.

"I've got to tell him carefully when the time is right. I'm sure you understand. I want to tell him myself and I will tell him, but I don't want to hurt him more than I have to."

There were tears in Mavis' eyes as she replied.

"How terrible about the beatings, my dear.

"Somehow you never think it will happen to your own flesh and blood, do you? And yes, of course, you must tell him yourself when the time is right. I understand.

"I'll tell Arnold and try to make sure he doesn't drop out any hints.

"It's not going to be easy. It's not going to be easy for either of you."

---ooo000ooo---

In the end it was Mary who inadvertently told Will.

It was six weeks after Will's return and Hetty was being sick in the bathroom one morning.

Will was concerned.

"Your poor mum. I don't know what's the matter with her."

Mary, whose greatest ambition at the age of five and a half was to become a 'Mummy', said, "She was sick like this before Dorothy arrived."

Will laughed.

"What do you mean? Who's Dorothy?"

Mary was eager to explain more.

"Dorothy's my sister. And Mummy was sick before she was born."

---ooo000ooo---

Hetty noticed that Will was pale and tight-lipped as she prepared Mary for school and set off with her but didn't think too much of it. He was quite often morose and shut in upon himself.

When she returned, however, he was waiting for her as she came in the front door, asking her sarcastically.

"And who's Dorothy?"

Hetty felt her legs go to water.

"How do you know about Dorothy?"

"Mary told me that you were sick in the morning before Dorothy arrived."

"Oh. Oh dear.

"Will, I was going to tell you straight away, but I've been waiting for the right moment and it hasn't come."

He glared at her.

"Well it's come now. Tell me now."

His voice was cold and hostile.

"You haven't asked me yet, how I got on while you were away. Well, I'll tell you."

"I had a telegram that said that you were *Missing, presumed dead,* did you know that?"

"Well about a year after the telegram came your parents invited me to go and live with them for a time because the bombing up here was so bad."

"People in the village were very kind to me and to Mary."

Will was vicious.

"They would be. But it sounds as if someone was too kind."

Hetty ignored his remark and continued.

"Then just after Christmas Mary became very, very ill with pneumonia and nearly died. Your mother and I sat up with her every night and it was touch-and-go for ages.

"When she started to recover, I was very low and upset and the local schoolteacher, David Holman, suggested that I might like to go for a walk in the sunshine to try to get my strength back."

"Your mum encouraged me to go because she understood how low I'd been."

"Oh yes. I remember him. A bit of a wimp—always off school for one reason or another.

112

"Go on... I can hardly believe this." He was sarcastic.

"I had got to know David very well over the months. He had involved me with helping at the church youth group and at the school and we had become good friends, enjoying each other's company. Well..."

"Go on, I'm fascinated," said Will grimly.

"Well I was very upset during that walk. I felt as if I'd already lost you and very, very nearly lost Mary and I just started crying and couldn't stop. David tried to comfort me...and somehow it all got out of hand and we made love."

"I see. Don't tell me you didn't enjoy that."

"It was an isolated incident," cried Hetty, "but it was enough and about six weeks later I found that I was expecting a baby. I was being sick in the mornings, as Mary has said.

"Your mum noticed too and it was all very difficult..."

Her voice faltered, while Will sat with his head in his hands.

She stumbled on.

"But David was very good and when we heard that you weren't dead—after more than two years remember—he took Dorothy to bring up on his own with his mother's help."

Her voice broke.

"I'm sorry, Will. I wouldn't have hurt you for the world. And I did really think I'd lost you; you know. It didn't feel as if I was cheating on you at the time..."

Her voice trailed off as Will's anger grew.

"But that's just what you were doing, isn't it? Obviously, your love for me didn't go very deep or you would never have done it."

"How could you be so cheap and nasty as to do it? How could you do it to me Hetty?"

He stood over her and glared at her, his fists clenched as if he would hit her.

Hetty's heart quailed.

"I'm sorry Will. It didn't seem like that then—and it still doesn't feel like that," she added bravely.

"Oh, so you're still in love with him, are you? Are you?"

"If so, you can go back to him. I don't want cheap, shoddy, second-hand goods, thank you! You little slut!"

Hetty gasped, but then shouted.

"I'm not. You don't understand! It's just one of those tragedies that happens in war. Nobody wants to hurt anyone else. It just happens."

"You must try to understand. It wasn't like that! And I won't be called names like that, either."

But Will's anger was growing.

"I don't think you've got any choice. You're just a cheap little slut who would screw anyone who spoke nicely to you."

"If that's all you think of me, then I'll go. David wants me, even if you don't."

"Oh, David wants you, does he?" Will mocked her.

"I could break every bone in his body! Does he know how much you've done it with me these last few weeks, what a willing bedfellow you've been?"

"Will he still want you if he knows all about that, then?"

"He does know all about it," said Hetty, sadly. "We couldn't bear the thought of you coming back to the sort of mess this is, and that's why David's taken Dorothy and I've come back to you."

"But if you don't want me, he does. I'll fetch Mary from school and we'll go today on the train.

"And he won't mind about the new baby either. He loves me, you see!"

Will mimicked her. "Oh, he loves you, does he? You're not taking Mary. And what new baby. What do you mean?"

"I'm being sick because I'm expecting another baby."

Hetty broke down and sobbed.

"I was going to wait until it had been confirmed by the doctor before I told you."

Will was silenced for a moment, but then his anger grew and grew and finally broke out as he went around the house breaking things.

He pulled down the curtains Hetty had made so carefully. He banged a chair so hard on the floor that the leg broke.

He pulled the cloth off the breakfast table, so that the cups and saucers all fell and broke.

Then he ran out of the house slamming the door so hard that the very walls seemed to shake.

Hetty sat and sobbed for a moment and then tried to tidy up a little before writing a note and leaving it on the kitchen table. It read simply.

I've gone to Peggy's for the day. I'll be back in time to collect Mary from school. Hetty.

As she sat on the bus for Hounslow, Hetty remembered a phrase from David's very first letter to her when he asked to be allowed to declare his love for her.

"My darling, the future is always unknown and is even more precarious than usual in wartime. I feel as if I've got enough love for you to fill your whole life even if Will returns... Although I can't tell you how much I long to hold you in my arms."

Hetty longed above all else for David's arms around her at that moment. What was she to do? Her future was certainly precarious.

If she turned to David now, she would not only lose Mary, but in all likelihood, she would lose the new baby too—Will's new baby.

Our baby is not going to be an inconvenience, David had said when Dorothy was on the way. *It's going to be wanted and loved.*

Why on earth had she gone back to Will? He didn't love her. He only wanted her and thought he loved her.

---ooo000ooo---

Peggy was kind but practical when Hetty got there.

"You must have expected something like that to happen. Will's always been a proud man and you've damaged his pride and self-respect badly—in addition to the damage his self-respect has already received in that wretched concentration camp."

"I know. But what am I to do now? He doesn't want me now that he knows about David. But he won't let me take Mary if I go to David and I imagine he'll want the new baby I'm carrying too. David looked into all the legalities of divorce when Dorothy was born and if I went to him, I wouldn't have a hope of keeping Mary—and how could I leave her?"

Hetty put her head in her hands and sobbed and sobbed.

Peggy plied her with tea and sympathy and waited for the sobs to subside.

"Will was angry and understandably so. Go back to him and try again.

"Collect Mary from school and take her home as usual as if nothing has happened. I think you'll find that he's recovered a bit by then, and he won't want to frighten Mary.

"But if he is still being violent, then get on the bus and come here for the night and we'll think again."

Then she added,

"In the meantime, there's a letter from David waiting for you. That will cheer you up.

"It might help you to write to him too to get all this off your chest if you can bear it.

"But don't put him in an impossible position, will you? It just wouldn't be fair on him."

David's letter, as usual, was full of Dorothy's latest doings. Now two-years-old, she was into everything, he said, and talking well enough to keep asking the dreaded question, 'Why?'

"It drives me mad," he said, *"but Penny tells me it is a phase they all go through."*

Hetty smiled as she read on.

I don't want you to think that because I talk a lot about Dorothy, I don't think of you. I do. I think of you all the time. I find that I am wondering as I wake up each morning what you are doing. And then I think back to what we were doing on this day a year ago when we were together. You were such fun to be with, Hetty. Dorothy makes us smile, of course, but all the joy has gone out of life without you and your lovely impulsiveness. I treasure every moment of it and I always will...

Hetty was comforted. Her letter back to him was more difficult. She needed to tell him what had happened, but she didn't want to grieve him unnecessarily.

I tried and tried to find a good moment to tell Will about you and Dorothy, but somehow it never came. He has been a very demanding husband physically which I think you would understand if you could see his back—he has been badly beaten—but he doesn't want to talk about his experiences or anything else. He's very shut in upon himself.

Mavis and Arnold were good when they came and said nothing, but in the end it was Mary who inadvertently told him today as I am being sick every morning again—and you know what that means! She told Will that I did it before Dorothy was born too! I'll spare you the full details of what happened after that! He was so angry it was terrible and so I came down here to spend the day with Peggy to try to give him time to recover.

Please don't grieve for me, David, but please think of me and pray for me—and Will. I find his sarcasm and anger so hard to bear and even more now that there is another baby on the way.

There seems to be no way out for us. I feel as if my heart— my whole body—is full of unshed tears, but as you know I'm tough and I'll survive. I long, above all else, for your arms around me...

---ooo000ooo---

In the event, Hetty found that Will was waiting at the school gate when she got there. His face was blotchy and his eyes were red and he wouldn't look at her.

"I saw your note and I was afraid you were going to take Mary off to your beloved David," he muttered sarcastically.

"No." Hetty answered simply.

"Not unless you want me to. I was going to collect her as usual and bring her home."

Then Will was forceful.

"Of course, I don't want you to take her away—or the new baby either. They're both mine.

"I've been to see a solicitor today and found out that they are legally mine and you will lose them if you leave me...so put that in your pipe and smoke it!"

"And what's more," he added. "I won't divorce you either, so that if you do want to go to your beloved David, you will have to live in sin!"

Hetty with great difficulty managed to hold back all the impulsive responses that sprang to her lips and busied herself instead with greeting Mary who was just running out of the school gate.

"Did you have a nice day?" She gave her a hug.

Mary's eyes were shining.

"Yes. And I've written a story all about my daddy coming home from the war and Mrs Coombs is so pleased with it that she's put it up on the wall."

"Well done!" Hetty was delighted.

"Do you want to come and see it?" She tugged at Will's hand.

"Yes, please."

So they all trooped into the school to read the story and then returned home with Mary as if nothing had happened, although Will still looked grim and carefully avoided looking at Hetty, pointedly giving all his attention to Mary.

Hetty felt herself shrivel inside and then suddenly knew that she was going to be physically sick.

She just got to the sink in time.

But this sickness wasn't like the morning sickness. It went on and on and she retched and retched until she had nothing left inside her and she was quite exhausted.

Will looked concerned.

"I want that baby. You'd better take care of it. It might be the son I've always longed for."

Finally, awkwardly, he added, "Is there anything I can do for you? Do you want me to get your parents or Peggy over?"

"No. I'll be all right in a minute if I sit down for a bit."

"I'll make you a cup of tea."

And so, an uneasy truce was established.

---ooo000ooo---

Hetty did keep the baby and in the course of time, the son Will longed for, was born. They called him Edward John, and Mary was delighted with her new brother.

Hetty had hoped against hope that the new baby would be the start of a new era for them, but it was not to be.

The baby did not improve her relationship with Will and she grieved that he was still so sarcastic and distant with her. He never lost an opportunity to point out how awful she had been to have an illegitimate child and to try to make her feel guilty.

Nor did he lose an opportunity to try to humiliate her in little ways, both by constantly criticising the way she ran the home and also by making disparaging remarks about her body and her ability as a lover.

It was her memories of David that kept her going.

She remembered their last evening together when he had poured out his love to her. She recalled every word and treasured them one by one.

Without them her self-confidence and hope would have deserted her entirely as she became bogged down in Will's constant, carping criticism.

And those other words of hers that David had so poignantly quoted back at her also kept her going.

What you forget in your grief is that you still need to give love as well as receive it.

I must somehow go on giving him love, she thought. *Perhaps in the end that will get through to him and heal him and he will be able to forgive me.*

She started to go to church again, enduring more sarcasm from Will as a result.

"What do you want to go there for? Are you hoping to go up in the world or something?

"I notice you haven't gone back to the Methodists. Afraid they'll find you out, are you?

"Afraid they'll find out about your illegitimate baby? I don't expect they want you there.

"And I don't think this Church of England you're attending will want you either when they find out."

Hetty sighed.

"Have you forgotten that the gospel is about love and forgiveness?"

"I get precious little of that here, so that's why I'm going. And anyway, I want our children to grow up to know and love God too, and that's also why I'm going, so that Mary can attend the Sunday School…"

Will was sarcastic.

"Well, don't expect me to come. There were plenty of people who prayed in the Concentration Camp, but it didn't do them any good as far as I could see.

"It's just a way of opting out."

David had reminded her in his last letter of a passage from the New Testament, when St Paul tells his readers he was 'holding them in his heart' when writing to the Philippians.

"I love the bit about holding you in my heart because I feel that I do that with you. And I do pray for you, my darling Hetty, just as you asked me to. I do pray that your love may abound more and more—in spite of all the difficulties. Above all, my darling, above all else don't get bitter. It is better to go on getting hurt than to become bitter. Oh, if only I could

be there to dry your tears. Somehow you'll just have to imagine that I am…"

---ooo000ooo---

Matthew Paul was born a year later.

Now Hetty was so busy that she had less and less time to visit Peggy to write to David and to receive his letters.

Meantime Will still hadn't improved. Indeed, his sarcasm and cutting remarks seemed to have become a way of life. She felt as if she could never get anything right.

The birth had not been an easy one and Hetty was exhausted and dreadfully down and depressed afterwards. Edward John was only a year old and just beginning to get into everything and now in addition she had a crying baby to cope with.

Mary was a great help when she came home from school, but she too soon got tired of crying babies.

And so did Will. What's more they interrupted what he regarded as his marital rights and he wasn't happy.

"Can't you do anything with them? I'm sure babies don't need to go on crying like this all the time.

"You're just no good with them, that's all. You've got no idea what to do. You're useless."

Hetty sobbed and sobbed.

She was finding it difficult enough to cope with the children, let alone with Will's constant demands on her.

She had to fight back the desire to scream and push him away when he put his hands on her and she often felt very sick when he entered her.

It wasn't rape. But it felt like rape to her as she wanted none of it and Will complained bitterly about her lack of response.

"I know, I'm useless. It's just that I'm always so tired.

"Other people have difficulty coping with three children too, you know," she rallied, "and with two babies so close together it's bound to be difficult."

"It's a good job you haven't got your fourth child here too, then, isn't it?" jeered Will.

Hetty put Edward and Matthew, one each end of the pram, helped Mary with her coat and satchel, and left to take her to school without a further word.

She knew that by the time she returned, Will would have left for his job with a local firm of accountants.

Once she had dropped off Mary, she turned the pram for home.

Suddenly she felt her tears coming and they wouldn't stop, so she turned into the church as she passed it and sat down in one of the back pews and wept with the babies in the pram beside her.

Then the words that David had quoted to her in that letter of nearly two years ago, now came back to her.

"It is right for me to feel thus about you, because I hold you in my heart, for you are all partakers with me of grace... And it is my prayer that your love may abound more and more with knowledge and discernment."

Somehow, she was able to turn it into a prayer.

Miraculously the two babies had both dropped off to sleep and Hetty felt fresh hope as she turned the pram towards home.

---ooo000ooo---

David was worried that he hadn't heard from Hetty for a long time and so one evening he telephoned Peggy. Tom, Peggy's husband, was home by this time, and he answered the phone and was puzzled by the request from a strange man to speak to his wife.

"Who is he?" he asked, as he handed the phone over.

Peggy quickly picked it up.

"The father of Dorothy—do you remember I told you what happened to Hetty during the war? I'll explain more later."

"Is Hetty all right?" were David's first words.

"I haven't heard from her for such ages. I know the baby was due and has probably come by now—but somehow, I can't stop worrying about her.

Is she all right?" he repeated.

Peggy sighed.

"Only just. She is very low after the birth of her second little boy—Matthew Paul, by the way, about a month ago now.

"Women do often get low and depressed after the birth of a baby, you know, especially when they have been in such quick succession as these two have been.

"Hetty's exhausted. She hasn't been to see me since long before the baby arrived, and when I telephoned her at lunchtime the other day, she was sobbing over the phone.

"In addition to the demands of the children, Will doesn't like the fact that she is so occupied with them that she has no time for him—and as you know he is a very demanding man."

David's heart sank. What a pig Will must be. The desolate expression on Hetty's face all those years ago in the cinema, flashed before him. If only he could do something—anything to help.

"If only there was a way, I could help her. I feel terrible that she is going through it like this."

"Peggy," he went on, thinking as he spoke, "is there a Guest House near you where I could stay for a week's holiday with Dorothy?

"Then perhaps Hetty and the children could come down to see you and Hetty could leave them with you for an hour or so while she came to see me.

"Do you think that would work? Or do you think it's a totally impossible idea asking for trouble?

"I just thought that seeing Dorothy might cheer her up— and I don't deny how much I'd love to see her too. What do you think?"

Peggy was thoughtful.

"Well, it might be asking for trouble. Let me think about it. I'll talk it over with Tom too and see what he thinks. I'll ring you back tomorrow evening if that's all right."

"Fine. I'll be in and waiting for your call."

Peggy rang off and explained it all to Tom.

"What do you think? Do you think it's a good idea or not?"

"It's a difficult one," Tom was speaking slowly.

"Of course, Hetty has a right to see Dorothy—and from what you've told me she hasn't seen her or David since Will returned. Is that right?"

"Yes, that's right.

"David came and stayed here several times during that last six months before Will came home, but he hasn't been since then."

"He is a nice man, Tom. You would like him. And he's not a philanderer."

"I think he and Hetty genuinely believed that Will was dead and that they would be able to marry in due course."

"He was very kind to me and the children when we went down there to help Hetty during the War when the baby was born. The children loved him."

"And as soon as he knew Will was coming back, he was careful just to support Hetty and not to make demands on her."

"In that case, I think a visit from him can only do her good—though, of course, it will be very painful for them both as well."

"It might be easier if you ask David and Dorothy over here for the day when Hetty comes."

And so, it was arranged that David and Dorothy should come and stay nearby.

Peggy phoned Hetty.

"You're coming down for the day next Wednesday."

"But…I don't think I can."

"By the time I've got Mary to school and the two boys ready, there's hardly any day left, and it's so difficult trying to get on and off the bus with two babies. I haven't got enough arms!"

"I'm not accepting any 'buts'."

Peggy unconsciously reminded Hetty of David's refusal to accept any either.

"Somebody will help you on the bus, I'm sure. You're coming! You need a break.

"And I'm sure Mary will be all right if you get a friend's mother to meet her from school and take her home to play until you get back.

"I expect she does go and play with other children sometime, doesn't she?"

"Yes, of course."

"Good. That's settled then.

"I'll make something for you to take back for Will's meal, so you don't need to worry about that either.

"I'll see you about ten o'clock on Wednesday—and don't be late, I've got a friend coming who wants to meet you."

"Oh, oh dear. I don't think I could cope with anyone else at the moment. Can't it just be you and me, Peggy? I can't cope with anyone else."

"All right. Don't worry. I know how you're feeling at the moment. I'll put them off. Just come."

But, of course, Peggy didn't put David off.

---ooo000ooo---

"Can I help you?"

Hetty was struggling to get off the bus the following Wednesday, with a pushchair, a bag and a baby on each arm.

"Yes, please." Hetty didn't look up. "Can you put the pushchair up for me?"

The bus conductor passed the pushchair off the bus and as Hetty climbed down she felt a hand on her arm, steadying her.

"Thank you."

She turned to see who had helped her and then gasped, going very white and feeling her legs buckle under her.

"David!"

He held onto her arm until she had recovered a bit.

"Let me put the little lad in the pushchair." He was practical.

"And give me your bag to carry. I imagine you're going to carry the baby, is that right?"

"Yes. Thank you."

She was embarrassed and could think of nothing to say.

"I've brought Dorothy to see you," David tried to cover her embarrassment.

"She's changing so much at the moment and she reminds me so much of you. We're staying nearby for a holiday and Peggy asked us across for the day. I hope you don't mind."

"No, of course not," Hetty was polite.

"Of course not. It's lovely to see you—and it will be good to see Dorothy too. It is kind of you to come."

"I hear the new baby—Matthew is it—is not very good. Is that right?"

"He doesn't sleep much at night, certainly.

"And what's more Edward still doesn't sleep through the night either. Sometimes I feel I've had no sleep at all—as soon as one stops crying, the other starts!"

David noticed her limp hair and how poorly she looked.

"Poor you. I remember what Dorothy was like when she was little and coping with two so near in age must be very difficult.

"I expect Will helps though, doesn't he, and Mary?"

"Mary's very good when she gets in from school. But I can't ask her to do very much and anyway she has homework to get on with now as well."

"And Will? Does he help?"

David's question was gentle but Hetty's lip trembled.

"Not really. He just thinks I'm a hopeless mother and should be able to manage better—and I expect he's right!"

"I see." David resisted the impulse to put his arm round her and pull her to him.

He did, however, put his hand on her arm again.

"Come on, give me that little one for a minute. I know that Peggy's got the kettle on ready and we're nearly there now."

126

Hetty handed Matthew to him and they were soon at Peggy's front door.

A small blond girl with large solemn eyes opened the front door.

"Dorothy! Well, Dorothy! Do you remember me then?"

"Sadly, I don't think she does. She was too young last time we came to remember you. But I think she will, next time."

Hetty couldn't take her eyes off her little daughter, while Dorothy herself was far more interested in the two baby boys who had just arrived, than in her mother.

"Can I hold the baby, please?"

"Yes, if you sit well back in that armchair and are very careful.

"Here he is. He's quite a weight, isn't he? Do you like babies, then?"

"Oh yes. I'd like us to have a baby too, but Granny says she's too old for babies now, so we can't have one."

"I see."

David at last saw the glimpse of a smile on Hetty's face, then laughed.

"She's quite cross with me about it. I think she thinks I ought to be able to have one all on my own."

Hetty laughed too.

"You'd certainly cause a stir if you did."

The morning passed happily with Hetty relieved of both babies by a combination of Dorothy, David and Peggy while the conversation ranged over all the fun they'd had together when Peggy and the children visited Wells when Dorothy was born.

In fact, Hetty relaxed so much that she actually dropped off to sleep.

"Leave her. You can see how much she needs it."

Peggy's advice was sensible.

Then after lunch she said that she would look after the babies with Dorothy's help while David and Hetty went for a short walk.

"It seems so strange to be walking with you again," said Hetty. "I can't believe it's really happening."

"Nor me. But it still feels very good, doesn't it?"

"Yes, I know. Everything has changed round us, but somehow, it's so comforting to know that you're still you and that Dorothy is growing up so beautifully in spite of everything.

"I only hope I can do as well with Edward and Matthew—in spite of being a hopeless mother," she ended on a sniff.

"Hetty, you haven't improved at all."

"You're still not believing in yourself and you're still regretting things."

"I don't know why I bother to write nice letters to you telling you how wonderful you are. You don't take any notice of them at all!"

Hetty smiled ruefully.

"Yes, I do. They're a lifeline. There are many times when I don't know how I would have managed without remembering what you've said in them."

"Will's been so damaged, you see. He never was much good at telling me he loved me, but now he finds it impossible to be anything but sarcastic and cutting.

"I try to tell myself that he doesn't really mean it and that underneath he's probably quite fond of me, and I manage to cope most of the time..." her voice trailed off.

David took her arm through his.

"I still think you're wonderful."

"And yes, you must go on making allowances for Will."

"I was reading something about those camps just the other day and they obviously specialised in humiliation, so it's not surprising that he's the way he is."

"I find it impossible to think how anyone can be like that to you, though. You're such a vital person and so loving and giving. He doesn't know how lucky he is."

Hetty wiped away a tear that had escaped and David put his arm round her shoulder.

"I cut this out of that article I was reading the other day," he said, putting a piece of paper in her hand.

"It's a prayer and it shows how very difficult it must have been for them all.

"It's typed, so you can keep it somewhere safe—or better still, learn it off by heart. I know it will help you, just as it helped me."

"Read it to me."

"I don't need to. I know it off by heart. Listen…

'Teach us to lay our course by a star we have never seen,
To dig for springs we may never reach.
O God, in the name of Jesus Christ, our inspiration
Give us the courage to wear out our hearts
After that which we may never attain.'"

---ooo000ooo---

Part Four

The next telegram arrived about three months later on a Tuesday.

Dorothy died early this morning from measles. Funeral Friday 2.30 pm. Please come. David.

When the post-boy arrived, Hetty was trying to get Will's evening meal ready, together with keeping an eye on Mary's homework and trying to cope with one baby toddling and the other crawling. She felt as if the bottom had dropped out of her world.

Somehow, she managed to continue with all the things she was doing, but her tears were spilling everywhere at the same time. Her beautiful child. What on earth could have happened. Being older, Maureen wouldn't have had the strength to sit up with her as much as she had with Mary when she was ill at the same sort of age. *I should never have left her,* she thought. *I should never have left her. It's all my fault.*

"What on earth's the matter with you?" Will was not sympathetic when he got home.

"It's not much fun coming home to a crying wife, I can tell you."

"I'm sorry. It's just that I've had a telegram…"

She handed it to him to read.

"He's got a cheek asking you to go to her funeral," was Will's only comment, having read it.

"I'm sorry for you, Hetty," he added, relatively kindly for him.

"Children don't usually die from measles," Hetty's voice broke. "There must have been a complication."

"I want to go to the funeral, Will. Somehow, I want to go to the funeral."

"Hetty, be sensible, you know you can't. And anyway, I don't want you to go. That bastard doesn't deserve to have you there."

"It's the death of a child and that child's funeral I'm talking about," cried Hetty.

"And yes, I'm sorry, but she is—she was—my child and the very least I can do is to go to her funeral."

"It won't make up for my neglect of her over the years. But I've got to go, somehow, I've got to go," her voice was verging on the hysterical.

"Well, you're not going. And that's an end to it. And for goodness sake pull yourself together or you'll upset the children."

"And where's my meal? I'm starving."

Hetty said no more and coldly served up his meal. But that night for the first time since Will had returned, she refused to make love to him.

Will was furious.

"How dare you deny me? You are MY wife, you know."

"I'm too upset. My daughter died today," sobbed Hetty. "I just can't do it. I'm sorry."

Eventually Will backed down and went off and slept downstairs, leaving Hetty to sob herself to sleep.

---ooo000ooo---

The next day as soon as Will had left for work, and she had taken Mary to school, Hetty telephoned Mavis and explained what had happened and Mavis was sympathetic.

"I'm so sorry, my dear. I had heard. It's such a tragedy. Poor David is distraught and Maureen looks terrible.

"I'm so sorry for you too. You must feel it so much. I wouldn't have had it happen for the world.

"Apparently she'd been ill for about two and a half weeks when a complication set in.

"She got bronchitis on top of the measles and she's asthmatic like David and they just couldn't save her. I'm so sorry."

A sob escaped from Hetty.

"I want to come to her funeral, but Will says I can't. Can you persuade him, Mavis?"

"Please, can you try? I really do need to come," her voice broke.

"Don't worry, my dear, I understand. Yes, of course you need to come.

"I'll ring Will tonight and see what I can do. I know it hasn't been easy for you, my dear, and I'm sorry."

"Thank you so much, Mavis. I can't bear the thought of not being there."

"What will you do with the children if you come?" Mavis was practical

"You could bring Mary and the two boys and leave them with me while you go to the funeral if you like."

"That might help Will to let me come, I suppose.

"Otherwise I was going to ask Peggy to have them for the day and night—as I won't get down to Wells and attend the funeral and get back home in the day."

"Thank you so much for being so understanding. I just hope you manage to persuade Will tonight."

In the meantime, Hetty telephoned Peggy and told her what had happened.

"Oh Hetty, that's terrible! Poor David! He was such a wonderful father. He'll be absolutely shattered. And you must be devastated too."

"I am. I don't know how to cope with it at all.

"I just know that I've got to get to that funeral somehow. What on earth will I do if Will goes on saying I can't go!"

"I don't know," Peggy sounded doubtful.

---ooo000ooo---

135

Will was still adamant when Mavis telephoned that evening and spoke angrily to his mother in response to her request.

"She's not going to the funeral and that's flat.

"If she comes, she'll meet that bastard at the funeral and I'm not having it."

"David is not a bastard, Will," his mother spoke mildly.

"Hetty and David thought you were dead or their relationship would never have started. And when they found out you were still alive, they acted very properly.

"Of course, we all regret what happened, but in spite of what you think, they have tried very hard to put it right."

"She's not coming and that's that." Will put the phone down on his mother.

Hetty could hear their conversation from the kitchen where she was sitting and her heart sank. What was she to do? Will came angrily into the room.

"My mother's been trying to persuade me to let you go to the funeral.

"Well, you needn't think that I'm going to give in to her persuasion because I'm not. You're not going."

Hetty said nothing, leaving the room a few minutes later to attend to Matthew who was crying.

---ooo000ooo---

Mavis telephoned her on Thursday morning with some good advice.

"Ignore him and just come anyway. I've been talking to Arnold and we agree that the local folk will expect you to be here.

"The news of Dorothy's birth and parenthood has, of course, leaked out over the years, but David has behaved so well about it all that people have accepted it now.

"I think you need to come not only for your own sake, but for David and his mother, as well. The local folk will expect it."

"What does Arnold feel about me leaving the children with you while I go to the funeral?" asked Hetty.

"He's fine about it. So leave Will a note tomorrow morning and just come."

"There's a train at 10 o'clock which will get you down here in time for the funeral. Arnold and I will meet you off it."

"Thank you, thank you so much. I'll see you on the platform at Wells tomorrow then."

---ooo000ooo---

Hetty rang Peggy and told her the plan.

"I'll come with you and stay with Janet or Penny. Then I can help you with the children on the train.

"Tom is going to take the day off so that he can drive us to the station. He's in the middle of doing some alterations to the bathroom and says he'll enjoy some time on his own to get on with it.

"That means he'll be here when the children get in from school and tomorrow's Saturday so they should all cope all right."

Hetty was relieved.

"That will be a help."

---ooo000ooo---

Friday dawned bright and sunny and as soon as Will had left for work, Hetty rushed round collecting overnight things for herself and the children.

Tom and Peggy arrived in good time in their Austin A30. She and the three children squeezed into the back and soon they were on their way to catch the train.

Before leaving, Hetty had left a cold meal out on a plate, ready for Will that evening, together with a note.

I'm sorry, but I had to go to the funeral in spite of what you said. I'm staying with your parents and Peggy's coming on the train with me to help me with the children. We shall get the 10.30 back from Wells on Saturday morning and Tom will meet us off the train. He'd like to drop Sarah and Peter off with you on his way to the station, if that's all right, as he won't get everyone in the car otherwise. He says he'll ring you tonight about it.

Love, Hetty

Will was furious when he got in, but as he ate his cold meal he gradually calmed down. There was nothing he could do about it anyway. The funeral would be over by now.

Perhaps this would be the end of it, he thought. *Perhaps that bastard, David, would vanish from his life now, and he wouldn't feel that he was always at the back of Hetty's mind.*

---ooo000ooo---

Meantime, Hetty and Peggy had been warmly welcomed in Wells, with Mavis and Arnold whisking the children off to the village.

Peggy and Hetty had a quick bite to eat with Janet before setting off for the funeral, which was to be held in the local parish church which David and Dorothy had attended.

She had been a member of the Sunday School and Hetty was amazed when she saw the letters and pictures the children had done for her.

David and Maureen greeted Hetty and Peggy outside the Church and they all went to sit together in the front pew.

The parson was kindly and brief and there was not a dry eye in the church at the sight of the tiny coffin.

Dorothy was to be buried in the churchyard and most of the congregation followed out there to hear the dreadful words of committal and see her lowered to her final resting place with the sprinkling of earth.

Hetty felt drained of all emotion as if she was simply going through the motions of what was required of her. Maureen sobbed quietly. David's eyes were dry and bleak.

Afterwards they went back to Maureen's house where Penny and Janet busied themselves handing round tea and cakes.

There were mementoes and memories of Dorothy everywhere. Hetty also found the photo she had taken five years ago now when she needed one to send to Will.

"Do you want a photo of Dorothy? I've a lovely one here."

"I'd love one, but it would be difficult at home."

"I'll have it," said Peggy. "Then you can see it whenever you come to see me."

David was polite and kind but withdrawn.

Hetty didn't feel she had spoken to him at all when the time came for her to leave to catch the bus back to the village.

She felt quite desperate about it, but there was nothing she could do. There were still visitors in the house and Maureen needed his support.

It was from Janet that she learned most. She sensed Hetty's need to talk and walked with her to the bus stop when she left to go back to Mavis and Arnold and the children in the village.

She told Hetty about Dorothy's illness and how hard they had fought to save her.

"David wouldn't leave her bedside day or night, though Maureen and I besought him to.

"What we did in the end was to take turns to sit in there with him so that he could snooze in the chair."

"She was just beginning to get over the worst of the spots when she suddenly developed bronchitis and with it became terribly wheezy and breathless.

"Poor David, he cursed himself that she had inherited his weak chest. We tried everything to keep her breathing."

The tears started to Janet's eyes and then to Hetty's in response.

"We had damp clothes hanging round the room to keep the air moist but in the end, she just slipped away almost without our noticing, it was so quick.

"David snatched her into his arms and tried to breathe into her, the tears pouring down his cheeks, but he couldn't bring her back."

---ooo000ooo---

When Hetty got back to Mavis and Arnold at 14 Wells Road, she found them quite exhausted.

"I'd forgotten what it was like to have babies in the house.

"Luckily Mary knew what to do at every stage and kept me right or I'd be in a terrible state. She must be a great help to you."

"She certainly is." Hetty gave Mary a hug. "I don't know what I'd do without her."

"Thank you so much, Mavis. I am so grateful to you for making it possible for me to go to the funeral. I don't think I could have lived with myself otherwise."

"How was David? And what about Maureen? Is she holding up all right?"

"Maureen looked exhausted, but otherwise she's all right, I think.

"It's David I'm worried about. I didn't really get a chance to talk to him—but that apart he seemed to be very withdrawn with everyone and he looked terrible."

"That's what I'd heard. Poor man. He's tried so hard with that child."

Soon the effort of getting all three children to bed excluded any further conversation and getting them up and ready the next morning was equally time consuming so that there was no time for further conversation before getting the bus to Wells to catch the train.

"Thank you again for everything." Hetty gave Mavis a hug. "It's made all the difference."

"Don't forget I'm here if you need me, will you? Have a good journey!"

All went smoothly and soon Hetty and Peggy were on the train returning to London.

"I do hope Will isn't too cross when I get back."

Hetty was apprehensive now that the train was nearing London.

"Tom will be there with Sarah and Peter so that should help."

And so, it turned out.

Tom duly met them from the train and when they got back to Harrow, they found Will enjoying himself with Peggy's children, as if nothing untoward had happened.

Hetty breathed a sigh of relief, but still dreaded being alone with Will that evening.

Amazingly for him, he was relatively kind and conciliatory.

"Has it helped you to get it out of your system, then, going to the funeral?"

Hetty gulped.

"I'm sorry I went even though you didn't want me to—but yes, it has helped.

"Somehow funerals are rather final…"

Her voice trailed off and she wiped away a tear.

"How was that bastard coping then?"

"I didn't get a chance to talk to him," Hetty was truthful. "So I don't really know—but he looked awful."

Will resisted the impulse to say, "Serves him right," and instead said thoughtfully, "I see."

Perhaps Tom had been right in what he had said in their telephone conversation on Friday evening.

---ooo000ooo---

It was six weeks later that Peggy got a telephone call from Maureen.

"I'm at my wit's end. David is in a terrible state. He's not shaving or looking after himself.

"He'll never initiate any conversation and only replies in monosyllables. He won't go out of the house but just sits staring into space.

"I don't know what we'll do when the summer holidays come to an end and he has to go to work again.

"We've all tried to rouse him out of it, and Penny and John have been marvellous—but all to no avail."

"And now I'm wondering whether you think there is any way in which Hetty could help?"

"I don't really like to ask as I know how difficult it has been for her, but I don't know where else to look for help now."

Peggy was horrified to hear all this and with many expressions of sympathy said that she would talk it over with Tom when he came in and also try to talk to Hetty on the phone.

She rang Hetty first and explained.

"Can you come down here tomorrow or Thursday so that you can write to him?"

"Yes, of course, I'll come tomorrow. But if he's in that sort of state I'm not sure that a letter will do much good."

"It's worth a try."

And so Hetty wrote:

I know that Dorothy's death must feel like the end of everything for you. It does for me too in a way—but I'm lucky I still have Mary and the boys. I wanted to talk to you so badly at the funeral, but there was no opportunity, was there? With the visible sign of our love gone in Dorothy's death, I wanted us somehow to remind each other of all our other special memories of our time together.

Do you remember quoting back at me more than once my words, "What you forget in your grief is that you still need to give love as well as receive it"? It may sound trite and annoying to you now, but nevertheless it still holds true. You have been so generous with your love first to me and then to Dorothy. But now when you want to give it, there's no one there. That's what's so hard.

I'm still here, of course, but you need someone there, with you, to love. How I wish it could be me, but that's impossible. As you know it's your love for me, supporting me by your letters, that has somehow made it possible for me to cope with

142

Will and has also helped me to find the love I need for the children. It's been a lifeline to me.

I would like to be a lifeline like that to you. But I can't be, because I can't be there with you.

I never thought I would say this to you, David, but because I can't be with you and because Dorothy's gone, you probably need to find someone else to love.

Our short time together was so loving and creative that you and I hoped to begin with, didn't we, to find a way back to each other through the maze we found ourselves in. We both know, I suppose, that can't happen now. You must realise, as I do at last, that Will and I are bound together for life by the children, whether we like it or not.

You once told me how selfish I was, do you remember? Well I'm trying so hard not to be selfish now. I can't keep you for myself, David, much as I would love to. It's not fair on you—and I've only recently realised that it's not really fair on Will either, however difficult he is. I can't keep a 'David-sized' piece of myself back from him.

We can neither of us go on crying for the moon because we're never going to get it. We'll just have to use our love—which was so special—as an inspiration for our other loves. As you know, that's what I've tried to do. The love you gave me back then has shown me how to cope with Will and I truly couldn't have managed without it.

I'm sure it was you who told me that true love is God-given, and it was certainly you who taught me that prayer from the Japanese Prisoner of War Camp. Do you remember how it ends? "Give us the courage to wear out our hearts after that which we may never attain."

I find this very hard to say, but I must say it or I won't be able to live with myself. Please find someone else to give your love to, David. There must be someone out there who needs it. Please, please find her and be happy for my sake. I cannot bear the thought of you without someone special to love.

There are others who need your love too, straight away now. Others who love you. Your mother has been marvellous and she must feel so desolated by all that has happened.

143

Then there are Penny and John—and Janet, who I know helped when Dorothy was so ill because she told me all about it. She still takes a great interest in all that happens to you. And there must be lots of others I don't know about as well.

However difficult it is, try to do just one or two small kind things for them each day to show you love them and gradually it will become easier to do more and more.

We'll never forget Dorothy. But by spilling out that love we had for her on other people, her short life won't have been wasted.

---ooo000ooo---

David received Hetty's letter two days later and it at last released the floodgates in him and allowed him to weep. Maureen was even more worried when he shut himself in his room and she heard his tears, but she wisely kept a low profile.

However, when John came round that evening to invite him out for a drink, David roused himself and smiled and accepted. Maureen breathed a sigh of relief as they left.

The next morning, when he came downstairs, shaved and looking better, he found Janet sitting at the breakfast table with Maureen.

Her eyes looked red, but she put her handkerchief quickly away when she saw David.

"I found this photo of Hetty and Mary and Dorothy tucked in the back of a book," she said tentatively, "and brought it along for you and Maureen."

David picked it up and smiled. Hetty was laughing, as usual, with Dorothy smiling up at her mother while she was hanging onto one of Mary's fingers.

"That's lovely," he said. "Thank you so much for bringing it along."

"I've got quite a lot more in among other photos in my album at home.

"You and Hetty and Mary and Dorothy were like my family when they were living with me, you know.

144

"I didn't bring the whole album round, as it's rather large and I didn't want to bore you. You're welcome to pop round sometime and have a look though."

"I'd love to."

David then remembered Hetty telling him about how badly Janet had wanted a child and how her sadness at her husband's death had been compounded by the fact that she hadn't had his child.

---ooo000ooo---

Hetty's telephone went just as she was giving Edward and Matthew their lunch. She balanced it on her shoulder as she went on shovelling food into Matthew and keeping an eye on Edward.

"I thought you might have the weather forecast on," said a voice she knew, teasing.

"David," gasped Hetty. "What's happened? Where are you calling from? Are you all right?"

"Yes, yes, don't worry. Have you a moment to talk now, or am I ringing at a hopeless time."

Hetty explained what she was doing.

"But they're relatively immobile while they're eating so it's not a bad time."

"You weren't listening to the weather forecast then?" David feigned disappointment.

Hetty laughed.

"The only times of the day I recognise are school times, mealtimes and bedtimes. Everything else is a frantic blur of trying to cope."

"It is so nice to hear you. Did you get my letter? I hope you understood…"

"That's why I'm ringing. Your letter was a colossal help.

"I was, as you realised, keeping my grief all to myself and almost hugging it. Your letter helped me to understand a bit more what was happening to me and to begin to get it out of my system."

"I'm glad. I felt so grieved that I had no chance to talk to you at the funeral and, like you I imagine, I needed to talk to someone about what had happened.

"Janet was wonderful. She took time to tell me about everything. That helped a lot. But it wasn't the same as talking to you."

"I know. And your letter brought all that back and reminded me what a wonderfully wise person you are and how I always loved talking to you and felt better afterwards."

"Me too, talking to you."

"That's why I had to ring. I hope you don't mind and I know I was taking a gamble, but suddenly I just had to hear your voice, had to hear you laugh."

Hetty was pleased that he couldn't see through the telephone the tears she was quietly wiping away.

"I meant the other bit in my letter too, about finding someone else to love."

David was silent for a moment.

"Hello—are you still there? I didn't mean that I don't still love you, you know. I do... Are you still there?"

"Yes, of course I am..."

"It's just..." Hetty was hesitant.

"It's just that it's never going to work out that way now, is it? We have to be realistic..."

Her voice trailed off.

"I know, I know. And that's partly why I telephoned. I needed to hear you say that as well as write it. Somehow hearing your voice makes the difference. And I still love you too, you know, and always will...it's just that as you say, it has to be different now.

"I wish we could at least be friends. I wish Will didn't hate me so. I wish so much that we could still see each other sometimes."

"Peggy's our only hope still and that will become more difficult as the children get older. I'm sorry Will is so jealous—but there it is.

"And he still won't talk about what he's been through. It must have been terrible."

"Letters then. We'll have to content ourselves with the occasional letter via Peggy. I couldn't bear us to lose touch altogether."

Hetty agreed

"No, we mustn't do that. I couldn't bear that either."

At that moment there was a loud scream. Matthew had tipped over his drink and was trying to climb out of his highchair.

"Hang on. Don't go away."

She mopped up, righted the children and returned to the phone. "Sorry about that!"

David laughed. "I suppose that's the way it's going to be from now on."

"'Fraid so. It's all gone here. But David, please promise you will telephone again like this if ever you're desperate, won't you?

"I'd hate you to feel that you couldn't. But you must be careful."

"I know. I won't do it again though, except in an emergency. Peggy's our best bet still, as you said. We'll go on writing through her."

He could hear the noise mounting in the background again.

"I think you're needed again. Goodbye my darling Hetty—and thank you."

"Goodbye, my darling David. Goodbye."

---ooo000ooo---

Six months later Hetty and Will received an invitation.

Mrs Maureen Holman requests the pleasure of your company at the marriage of her son, David, to Mrs Janet Smith, at Wells Parish Church and afterwards at The Rose & Crown Hotel, Wookey, on Saturday 3rd July 1949 at 2 pm.

Will opened the envelope, which arrived on a Saturday morning.

"They've got a cheek to ask us. Who does he think he is? Does he think his new wife will want to meet his former mistress!"

"Don't be like that. Janet Smith was wonderful to Mary and me. We went to live with her when I discovered that I was expecting Dorothy. I don't know how we would have managed without her."

"Her husband was lost in the war. Like you he was posted as *Missing*—but unfortunately there wasn't a happy ending for her. It was only three months until his body was found.

"I'm delighted David is marrying her. I hope they'll be very happy."

Will looked at her for a long time.

"Are we very happy, Hetty? I'd like us to be."

"So would I."

Hetty smiled steadily at him and for once Will pulled her to him and kissed her quite tenderly.

---ooo000ooo---

Part Five
1965

The NEXT telegram arrived as Hetty was sweeping up the leaves the large Plane Tree in the nearby park had deposited all over their garden. She smiled as she remembered how much the boys had enjoyed doing this when they were little, particularly delighting in the bonfire that followed.

The Guy Fawkes Bonfires came at about the same time, but somehow the bonfire of leaves was especially theirs and it was their job to feed it with leaves and keep it going— besides making sure that it didn't get out of control. They had always got themselves quite filthy, she remembered as well as smelling of damp and smoke and sweat.

She thought the telegraph boy must be going next door when he parked his bike against the fence, but then he appeared to change his mind and came towards her.

"Mrs Thomas?"

"Yes, that's me."

"I've got a telegram for you."

Hetty snatched it from him, her thoughts on Mary, who was married and living in Richmond, Eddie in his third year at University and Matt just coming to the end of his National Service. At least Liz was still living at home. Her hand trembled as she opened it.

David died last night. Bronchitis. Funeral 1 pm Thursday. Please come. Love Janet

Hetty trembled and hung on to the gatepost.

"Is there any reply, Miss?"

"Yes, just say *So sorry. I'll be there at Funeral. Love, Hetty.* Have you got that?"

He read it back to her and she went indoors to get her purse to find the ten shillings payment he asked for.

Having paid him she turned and walked slowly into the house and sitting down heavily on a chair in the kitchen, stared into space.

David.

He couldn't be dead...

He had always been there.

His marriage to Janet hadn't changed anything.

She had only read the last letter from him and Janet two weeks ago when she had spent the day with Peggy.

Hetty had always known that he—they—were there if she needed them.

And now he wasn't.

And worst of all, she hadn't had a chance to say goodbye.

She felt bereft and a great loneliness overcame her.

---ooo000ooo---

There hadn't been a lot of contact over the years since his marriage. There had been sporadic letters, holiday postcards, Christmas cards, all via Peggy and mainly full of family news.

They told of the birth of David and Janet's first child—a little boy they called John and then the birth of their daughter, Madeleine. She was born in the same month as Will and Hetty's second daughter, Elizabeth, who was now sixteen and doing her 'O' levels. They had exchanged photos then, Hetty remembered. John and Madeleine were beautiful children, smiling and happy.

There had been one meeting. David and Janet had come to stay for a few days with Peggy and Tom, together with their children, about ten years ago. Hetty had gone down there for the day, with Eddie and Matt and Liz.

It had not been a great success. Eddie and Matt had soon got bored, although Hetty remembered David's valiant efforts to keep them happy and include John in their games. The two little girls had got on well, on the other hand, and had a happy time together.

Any sort of private conversation had been impossible and Hetty had spent most of the time talking to Janet and Peggy about the children, while David kept them occupied.

Worst of all, Will had heard about the meeting and been furious.

"I thought you'd got over that bastard," he said when he realised who they had spent the day with at Peggy's.

"You didn't bother to tell me who you were going to see, did you, or suggest that I should come down too?"

"I didn't think you'd want to meet him. You've always been so rude about him," Hetty was defensive.

"It's nine years since they got married, you know. And they seem very happy. There's no need for you to go on being so horrible about him."

"Then there's no need for you to meet them, either. I can't think that Janet will be very pleased to be in the same room as her husband's former lover."

"It's not like that," Hetty remonstrated.

"Janet and I were good friends when we were living there and David was keeping an eye on us and nothing has changed. We're still good friends.

"I'm sure she knows that she can trust David and trust me. We all supported each other through a difficult time. But perhaps you can't understand that."

"No, I can't. I can't trust people like that. Don't see them again, please."

Hetty had sighed and the conversation had ended there.

She didn't mention it in her next letter either, realising that there probably wouldn't be another meeting for years anyway—if at all.

And now he had died and there hadn't been another meeting.

Yes, that had been their last meeting, Hetty thought now. *Ten years ago!*

He had still looked good then. And he and Janet had looked happy and comfortable together.

She had noticed his carefulness in looking after her and his children—and although she had been glad for them, she had found it hard not to be jealous.

Will never seemed to notice how she was feeling, or if any of the children were unhappy. He only noticed them if they stepped out of line in some way.

And now David was dead. Poor Janet. Poor John and Madeleine. They must be eighteen and sixteen. Very young to lose their father. And he must have been such a good father too.

And Maureen. Poor Maureen. As far as she knew, Maureen was still alive. She must be desolate. How terrible to lose your son like that. Janet would look after her, Hetty knew that, but poor Maureen. She had been so good to them all.

I'd better tell Peggy, she thought dully. *She may want to come to the funeral with me.* She picked up the telephone and explained to Peggy what had happened.

"Oh Hetty," said Peggy. "How terrible. Those poor children! Poor Janet! And Maureen—poor Maureen!"

"Hetty, I just can't believe it. He's always seemed so solid somehow, as if he would always be there. I just can't believe that he's not."

"Are you all right?" asked Peggy. "I know you loved him."

"Yes, I'm OK, though I feel as if nothing will ever be really all right again."

"I know what you mean. Thursday, you said, didn't you? The funeral's going to be on Thursday. You're going to go, are you? What about Will? Does he mind?"

"I don't care whether Will minds or not. I'm going to the funeral.

"I don't think he'll try to stop me this time as he did when Dorothy died. I imagine Mavis and Arnold will be on my side again.

"That's a point, I'd better tell them, in case they haven't heard."

"I don't imagine Will will want to come with you at any rate. Would you like me to come with you?"

"I'd love that. Somehow, you've been in all of this mess for me, Peggy and I do appreciate it.

"It's made all the difference being able to share it with you and it will make all the difference if you can come to the funeral with me too.

"I am sure it will help Will to accept that I'm going as well if he knows that you are with me."

"That's settled then. What time did you say it was?"

"One o'clock. That may mean that we can get there and back in the day. I'll check the train times."

They talked about a few more details and then rang off.

Then Hetty telephoned Janet.

John picked up the phone.

"Hello. Wells 2395."

Hetty's heart leaped. It was David. It must all be a mistake. But then she realised…

"Is that John? It's Hetty Thomas here. I've just had your mother's telegram about your father's death."

"Oh yes, and she's had your telegram back. She's so pleased that you are coming to the funeral."

"How is she? Can I speak to her?"

"Yes, of course. I'll get her for you."

"Hello Hetty," it was Janet's voice.

"Janet, I'm so terribly sorry! I just can't believe it and I'm sure you can't either."

"As when Dorothy died, it was so quick in the end that we didn't have time to take it in."

Janet sounded heartbroken.

"This was his second bout of bronchitis in quick succession, so I suppose he hadn't had time to build up his strength in between.

"Almost before we knew what was happening it had turned into pneumonia.

"I'd left the room to telephone the Doctor to say that he was worse and when I returned, he was dead.

"Oh Hetty, I didn't even have a chance to hold his hand or say goodbye."

155

"Oh, how terrible. That must be so hard for you. And the children? Are the children all right?"

"We're all crying together. And Maureen too. She's here as well. We all feel as if the bottom has dropped out of our world."

"I know," Hetty's voice was sad as her own tears at last began to fall.

"And John is trying so hard to be the man. That's what breaks my heart as well.

"Why don't you stay the night after the funeral?" she added.

"Peggy is coming with me and we planned to go and come in the day to make things smoother for the men."

Hetty, bit her lip as she realised what Will's reaction would be.

Soon their conversation ceased and Hetty put her head in her hands and wept.

When Liz arrived home from school at 4.30, she was worried to see her mother had been crying.

"Are you all right, Mum? What on earth's the matter?"

Hetty explained that an old friend had died.

"You won't remember, but you met him about ten years ago, when we went down to Peggy's for the day.

"I had you and Matt and Eddie with me and he and Janet had two children, John and Madeleine. Madeleine is the same age as you and you enjoyed playing together."

"I remember," cried Liz. "I really liked her and we had fun together. I think I remember her parents vaguely too and her brother. It's her father who has died, is it?"

"Yes. He and Janet are old friends from during the war.

"I'm going to the funeral on Thursday and Peggy is coming with me, as she knew him well too.

"Do you think you can get your father's evening meal that day for me? I'll leave everything ready for you."

"Of course, I can, Mum." Liz was smiling. "And you don't have to leave everything ready either. I'll manage. It will be good for me. I am doing Home Economics at school, you know."

"I know how good you are. That's settled then," Hetty gave her a hug

"And cheer up, Mum. I don't remember seeing you as upset as this. Was he a very great friend then? If so, it's funny that we didn't see more of them."

Hetty sighed.

"It's a long story. Yes, they were great friends. David and Janet were very good to Mary and me during the war, when Dad was in the Concentration Camp.

"We've always kept in touch by letters, but somehow Wells has been too far away for more than that."

"But that's not far from Gran and Granddad. We could have visited David and Janet when we visited them."

"It wasn't as easy as that. I'll explain one day."

Liz sounded rather puzzled.

When Hetty told Will later that evening, he only just managed to restrain himself from being sarcastic as Liz was present.

"Hmph. Do you really have to go? I'm sure nobody's going to miss you."

"I want to go and Peggy is coming with me."

"Janet was so good to me during the war that the very least I can do is to go to her husband's funeral." She was conscious of Liz in the room, listening.

"All right, all right, I know what a do-gooder you are. You'll have to go then."

---ooo000ooo---

Appropriately somehow, it was a cold miserable winter's day for David's funeral. All went well with Hetty and Peggy's travelling plans and they arrived at St Barnabas' Church, Wells, in plenty of time, so they were amazed to find that there was hardly a seat left.

The church was packed—and it was one o'clock on a weekday.

"I suppose some people must have come in their lunch hour," Peggy whispered, "but I never expected to find it as full as this."

Hetty spotted Mavis and Arnold sitting near the back, and she and Peggy went to join them.

"It's so good to see you. I never expected as many people as this, did you?"

"David has really put himself out to help people over the years," said Mavis, "so I'm not surprised.

"As you know he ran the Youth Club in the village, when you were there, and after he and Janet were married, he started one up at the Church here."

"The young people loved him, and that meant that their mums and dads and grans and granddads did too. He really put himself out for people."

"That's wonderful. I'm so glad."

Although sad, the service was also inspirational and though people were crying quietly, they were smiling through their tears.

The clergyman had obviously been a great friend of David's and was able to speak of him with real personal insight.

"One of David's favourite passages in the New Testament," he said towards the end of his address, "was from Philippians 1. It was this:

"'It is right for me to feel thus about you, because I hold you in my heart, for you are all partakers with me of grace… And it is my prayer that your love may abound more and more with knowledge and all discernment.'

"He once told me that he liked to feel that he was holding people in his heart and that this was his daily prayer for himself, as well as for those he loved."

Hetty recognised the passage that David had quoted to her all those years ago, when Will first returned and things were so difficult, and although up to that point she had restrained her tears for the sake of Mavis and Arnold, she could hold them back no longer and let them run down her face unchecked.

After the service Janet, John, Madeleine and Maureen were standing in the porch to greet folk as they left.

It was a long, slow progress to get to them, but when they did Janet greeted Hetty with open arms and their tears mingled as they wept briefly on each other's shoulders.

"We must talk sometime," said Janet. "It is so good to see you. I'm so glad you could come."

Then Peggy had an idea.

"Why don't you come and stay for a night with me and then Hetty could come too and you two could talk. You won't feel like it for some time yet. But later on, it might do you good."

"That's a nice idea. Thank you."

She then went on to remind John and Madeleine who Hetty and Peggy were.

"Do you remember going to stay with Peggy? It was ten years ago now. We all knew each other well during the war."

"I do."

"So do I. I played with a nice little girl I remember."

Maureen was equally welcoming.

"Now your children are older, couldn't you come and stay sometime?"

"That would be nice. I'd love to." However, Hetty knew in her heart that Will would never allow it.

"We must all keep in touch somehow," said Maureen.

---ooo000ooo---

True to her word, Peggy telephoned Janet three months later and asked her to stay.

She came on her own, having left her children to fend for themselves with Maureen keeping an eye on them.

Hetty got an early bus and they had a full day together, firstly all three of them talking about their time together.

Then Peggy suggested that Janet and Hetty should take advantage of the fine weather and go for a walk.

"I badly wanted to talk to you, Hetty. I know we haven't been in touch much these last few years, but I didn't want you to think that David—that we—had forgotten you.

"The photograph you had taken with Mary all those years ago, to send to Will, is still on the sideboard among all our family photos, because we always felt as if you were part of the family."

Hetty was silent for a moment.

"Did you never resent me? It must have been difficult for you."

"No. I loved Dorothy as you know and I too was devastated by her death. She had in some ways become the child I'd never had.

"Perhaps you didn't know how much I helped with her. I was a daily visitor and babysitter.

"Somehow our common grief for her created a bond between David and me which gradually drew us together. And because you were Dorothy's mother and my friend, you were included in that.

"I know I've got a lot else to thank you for too. David showed me your letter to him after Dorothy died.

"It had given him so much hope, he said, and it had shown him that there were other people he wanted to give love to— like me.

"He told me about the words you kept quoting at each other, *'What you forget in your grief is that you still need to give love as well as receive it.'* I've remembered that such a lot since he died too."

"Thank you, Janet. Thank you so much for telling me that. You are such a generous person."

"By the sound of it, it's you who have had to give, and give and give again—to Will.

"David told me how he had been tortured and how difficult and demanding he was. It can't have been easy for you."

"No. He does love me, I think, but he can never let himself express that love. Something inside him holds him back and sarcastic remarks come out instead.

160

"It used to hurt me terribly—that's why David's letters and support was such a help. But I suppose I've learnt to live with it now.

"I do dread what it will be like when Liz leaves home, though. She is the last one. The others have all fled the nest now.

"While she is there, Will restrains himself. His sarcasm to me is mainly uttered out of earshot of the children and they love him.

"I'll find it more difficult to manage when they've gone. Apart from anything else, he misses them all so much—and I'm no substitute."

"Can we write freely now that David is dead?"

"I don't see why not. It's easier through Peggy though, as Will sometimes takes it into his head to open and read my letters, so nothing is private. Any letter you send to me has to be one that he can read too."

"I see," said Janet. *Poor Hetty,* she thought. *How terrible to feel that there was no freedom of expression in your own home.*

"You could telephone sometimes, though. Will is at work most weekdays and lunchtime is a good time to ring."

"I'm afraid I can't ring you very much, though, as he keeps an eye on that too. I can pretend its Mavis and Arnold I'm ringing once or twice, but after that he would smell a rat."

"I'll ring you then. It certainly would be nice to natter sometimes."

---ooo000ooo---

It was five years later that Will was taken ill. To begin with, it was hardly noticeable and he tried to hide it, but Hetty soon realised something was wrong. He had developed cancer and discovered that it was incurable and that he hadn't long to live. What was worse, was that he was absolutely furious about it.

"How could this happen? As if I haven't had enough to cope with already. How could this happen!"

161

"I know." Hetty knew the sort of row that would follow and being totally unable to do anything about it, her heart sank.

"No, you don't know," he was shouting. "How could you know? Don't you dare patronise me!"

She was silent then, as he ranted on.

"And when are the children coming to see me then? I suppose you've told them what's happened?"

"I've said you're not very well, that's all. But I will tell them now if you'd like me to. I thought you might want to tell them yourself."

She telephoned the children in turn that evening.

Mary, who now had a little girl of her own, Joanne, promised to come over the very next day. "If you're sure that Joanne won't tire Dad."

"No, he loves to see her."

Eddie was now working in the city and had a flat in central London which he shared with Matt, who was a journalist and working on a motoring magazine, and two other friends. He was horrified.

"That's terrible! Isn't there anything that can be done for him? What about chemotherapy. Cancer can often be cured these days, it's not always terminal."

"I know, and we've looked into all this, but I'm afraid your dad put up with it too long without saying anything, so that there's now very little that can be done and it will get progressively worse.

"He does love to see you, though, so any time you can spare to come and see him will help a lot."

"Of course. I'll get down as often as I can—starting this coming weekend. Is that OK? I'm sure Matt will come too if he's free. Do you want to talk to him as well?"

"Yes, please and I shall look forward to seeing you at the weekend."

Matt had a soft heart and Hetty's heart bled when she heard the crack in his voice and the worry.

"Isn't there nothing we can do?"

"Not unless there's some wonderful medical advance. It certainly doesn't look like it at the moment."

"He would like time with you all, though, before it gets too bad. Later, if I know him, he won't really want you to see him."

"I see. I'll be down at the weekend too."

Liz was the worst. She was in the last year of a Teacher Training Course in Bath and Hetty had quite a job trying to get hold of her. She spoke to her friend, Jane, who promised to get her to ring back.

"What's up?" She rang that evening.

"It's your father. He's not very well at all."

"Oh Mum! Oh dear! Do they know what's wrong?"

"He's got cancer and he put up with it too long before saying anything and now it's gone too far and there's nothing that can be done."

"Does that mean he'll die?" Liz sounded fearful

"Yes, eventually, but I'm afraid it is a fairly long miserable process. I know it will be hard for you, but any time you can spend up here would really help. I'll send you the train fare."

Hetty could hear Liz crying on the other end of the phone.

"I can't come this weekend. We've got full-scale rehearsals all weekend for the College production of Hamlet. As you know, I'm playing Ophelia, so I can't miss them.

"I had so hoped you could come to it," she sobbed, "and Dad—but I suppose that won't be possible now."

"It should be possible. Perhaps we can come and stay at a hotel nearby somewhere, so it's not so tiring for him.

"He'd love to come, I'm sure. It's coming on quite soon, isn't it? We'll come to it somehow."

Will was delighted at the prospect of seeing his daughter in her College production—and so it was organised.

---ooo000ooo---

Hamlet was a resounding success and Liz was an ethereal Ophelia. Will was so proud of her and delighted when she came around to spend the next morning with them at the hotel, before their return to Harrow later in the day.

Hetty thought that perhaps Will might like Liz to himself for a bit and so made an excuse to do some shopping while they talked, knowing how much father and daughter meant to each other.

Hetty was the sole recipient of his anger and sarcasm and had worked hard all her married life to hide it from the children and to make sure that they appreciated their father's good qualities and didn't learn about the bad.

"Dad, I can't bear what is happening to you," Liz burst out to her father.

"It seems so unfair. I cannot bear it!"

"I know. I always felt that I'd had my fill of nasty things by the end of the war, what with the Concentration Camp and one thing and another."

"You've never told us about that. Tell me about it now. Was it terrible?

"You and Mum were married before the war, weren't you, and Mum was on her own with Mary all through the war.

"That must have been terrible for her too. Tell me about it all."

And for once, Will started to talk about it all.

But suddenly he found he wasn't talking about the Concentration Camp, although he told her briefly about it. Instead all his anger and resentment about Hetty's so-called 'desertion' during the war, about the birth of Dorothy and about 'that bastard David' was poured out.

"You, none of you, knew any of that before, did you? Well it's about time you knew that your wonderful mother isn't quite as perfect as she seems."

Liz was absolutely horrified. She had never heard any of this before. They none of them had.

Will had, in fact, forbidden Hetty to talk of it to the children and even Mary, who of course remembered some of it, had been sworn to secrecy and asked to forget it.

"Why didn't you tell us before?"

"I was too ashamed of her. Too ashamed, after all I'd gone through, to think that she had preferred someone else to me."

"How long were you gone for?"

"Three years. Only three years. You'd have thought she could have waited three years, wouldn't you—and she had a baby too."

He was really working himself up now and Liz was heartbroken as she saw the tears suddenly pouring down his cheeks.

She put her arms round him.

"I'm so sorry, Dad, I'm so sorry. I never knew. We, none of us, did. Poor you!"

"How could she do that to you? How could she! And then not to tell us about it!

"What happened to the baby?"

"It died after a few years. Its father looked after it and it died—and serve him right—the bastard."

And he started to sob even more, so that when Hetty returned she found both Will and Liz in a dreadful state.

"What's all this? What on earth's the matter?"

"I should have thought you knew," Liz's voice was cold.

"Knew what? Of course, I know about the cancer if that's what you mean."

"No, I don't. I mean what happened during the war. How you broke Dad's heart. That's what I mean."

"Oh. He's told you about that, has he? I see."

"It's about time we knew," Liz was sobbing again. "How could you! Why didn't you tell us?"

Hetty's heart quailed within her, her legs trembled and she sat down suddenly.

She didn't tell them because Will had forbidden her to— and now he had changed the rules. If she told Liz this now, it might turn her against her father in the last few months of his life. She couldn't do that.

"It's not as straight forward as you think," she said finally, the tears running down her cheeks as well.

"No, it certainly isn't, I can see that," Liz was vicious. "I don't know how you could do it. Poor Dad!"

165

Hetty turned away.

"I'll go and pack. We must get going as soon as we've had lunch."

---ooo000ooo---

Three weeks later Liz decided to go to Wells—only a bus ride from Bath—to see if she could find the grave of the baby who died and a little more of what happened. She phoned her grandparents, Mavis and Arnold, to see if she could stay Saturday night with them and they were, of course, delighted.

It didn't take her long to find the cemetery and the small grave.

Dorothy Holman, the inscription ran, *died of measles at the age of four. Given us to love for a short time only.*

Liz stood looking at it for a long time, thinking.

"My goodness. I suppose she was my stepsister. But how could my mother do it."

She was still angry with Hetty and their farewells after Will's revelations had been brief and cold, with no further explanations offered.

Then she saw the grave next to that of Dorothy.

David Holman
Departed this life 20 November 1968.
He loved much and was loved by all.

Suddenly a great fury overtook her as she read the inscription.

"He loved much and was loved by all, was he? Well they couldn't have known very much about him to write that, could they?"

"How could you?" She was shouting at the top of her voice.

Then she remembered how her father referred to him.

"You bastard, bastard, bastard..." Still shouting, she stamped on the grave.

"Hey," a voice shouted in reply. "What do you think you're doing?"

A very angry young man was running towards her.

"What do you think you're doing," he repeated as he reached her.

"That's my father's grave you're stamping on.

"What do you think you're doing?"

Liz burst into tears.

"I'm sorry. It's just..." her voice trailed off.

"I didn't know it was your father," she added miserably.

John looked at her and his anger began to melt away. She was fair and slender and her eyes were large with tears.

"Why don't you come over here and tell me what it's all about," he said, indicating a nearby bench put there in remembrance. He proffered a clean handkerchief as Liz wiped her nose on her sleeve.

"Wait a minute, I know who you are, I think... I think you're one of Hetty's daughters, aren't you?"

Liz looked at him in amazement.

"How on earth do you know?"

"My parents talked about Hetty a lot. And I think I may have met you once a long time ago when we were all children, at your Aunt's house.

"You played with my sister, Madeleine, I believe. Is that right?"

"Probably," Liz was amazed. "I haven't got a very good memory."

"But you haven't told me why you're so upset," said John.

"My father's very ill with Cancer. And I'm a bit upset, that's all."

"I see, but why would that make you stamp on my father's grave? I loved him very dearly, you know, and that hurt me a lot."

"If your parents talked to you about Hetty—about my mother—did they tell you what happened, what she did, during the war?"

"Yes, of course. We knew all about it."

"Well, we didn't. I've only just begun to find out.

"As I told you my father's very ill with Cancer and he and I are very close and he was very upset one day and told me. We, none of us, knew anything about it before."

"I begin to see. So, you've only heard your father's side of the story, is that it?"

"Isn't that enough? I know that my mother was unfaithful to my father—deserted him—when he was in a Japanese Prisoners of War Camp. Can you believe it?!"

John was silent.

"And as if that wasn't enough, she got pregnant by this B...man—your father I suppose."

Liz's indignation was mounting again.

John felt himself beginning to get angry again too.

"I don't think you begin to understand anything about it. This is my father you're talking about, remember?"

Liz looked rather abashed.

"I'm sorry. I suppose I'm really very confused about it all...only my father was so upset. He was crying you know. Sobbing. Sobbing because my mother was unfaithful to him all those years ago.

"I love him so much and I can't bear to see him upset like that especially now that he's got cancer and is not going to recover."

She blew her nose hard on John's handkerchief.

"I'm sorry. I shouldn't be burdening you with all this—a total stranger. I don't know what I'm thinking about. I'd better go away and leave you alone."

And she began to rise, as if to leave.

"Hey, haven't you been listening to me at all?

"As I've only just finished telling you, I'm not a total stranger and in fact I regard you as part of the family—because that's how my parents looked on Hetty."

"They were all so fond of each other. And anyway, Dorothy was half-sister to both of us, so that must help."

"Were they…was she…? I find it hard to believe, you know. But you don't have to be kind to me you know. You shouldn't be bothering."

John half smiled.

"But I want to bother. I can't let you go away thinking my father was horrible, apart from anything else, because it sounded as if you were calling him names back there."

He didn't give Liz a chance to reply.

"He was a kind man. Madeleine and I both know about what happened between Hetty and my dad. Mum and Dad never made any secret of it."

"But didn't your mum mind?" Liz was astonished.

"You mum lived with my mum, with Mary, when she was expecting Dorothy. They became great friends. Then later on, after Dorothy had died, Dad married Mum."

"Oh." Liz was confused by all this new information.

"Come on."

"Come on where?" Liz was rather alarmed.

"Come home with me and meet my mum. She'll tell you all about it.

"She'll be so pleased to meet you, as well…that is so long as you don't call my dad names.

"I won't tell her you stamped on his grave."

There was a hint of a smile.

"I'm sorry. I shouldn't have done that. It was a terrible thing to do."

"Yes, but the heat of the moment and all that… Are you going to come and meet my mum then?"

"I don't think I can. I still feel so mixed up and it wouldn't be fair."

"Well, why don't you come and have a bite of lunch with me. You look half-starved and there's a cheap café not too far from the Cathedral Close."

"I am hungry, I suppose."

"Good, that's settled then. Come on."

He then began to talk cheerfully about other things to give her time to compose herself, before asking her how she came to be in Wells.

"I'm at Teacher Training College in Bath and came across to see my grandparents who live in a village nearby."

"Oh, you mean Mavis and Arnold."

Liz was astounded again.

"Don't tell me you know them too?"

"Everyone knows everyone else in a small community. Your mum sat with Mavis and Arnold at my father's funeral. They were there too, you know."

"Oh, did they know what had happened then?"

"Yes, and like you they were furious at first, but in the end they came to accept the inevitable and realised that both my father and Hetty had done their very best to put things right in time for your dad's return.

"They hadn't thought he would return; you see. Your mum had had a telegram telling her that your father was 'presumed dead' about eighteen months before she met my father.

"They were just friends at first for a long time and then one day your mother was very upset because Mary had been very ill—and that was when they began a closer relationship."

"Oh, you make it sound all so natural and reasonable."

"Well, I believe in the circumstances that it was natural and certainly understandable."

"Perhaps I should come and meet your mum sometime. But even so, I still don't understand why Mum couldn't say 'No' to your dad."

"How old are you?"

"I'm twenty-one, nearly twenty-two. Why do you ask?"

"Well, can you remember the things that were really important to you eighteen months ago, the things that made you laugh and cry?

"Your mum was only a year older than you when all this happened, you know. She had been on her own for over eighteen months and trying to cope with a small child as well.

"I think you're too hard on her.

"Anyway, I don't think any of us can really understand what it felt like during the war.

"People got married in a hurry because they thought their boyfriend or girlfriend might get killed. There was an urgency about that I think it's difficult for us to understand."

"You've obviously thought about all this a lot. But if it was understandable for Mum to behave the way she did, how about your dad? Wasn't he just taking advantage of her dilemma?"

"Dad did tell me that he blamed himself for what happened. But he said that he was very inexperienced and he didn't realise how quickly things could get out of hand."

"He was warning me in a way, I suppose. He was warning me to find out as much as I could before getting involved with anyone."

"That's another thing which it is hard for us to understand, I think," he went on, "how innocent they were.

"There was no teaching about sex at all. I know we don't have very much, but they had none and they had to find out how powerful it is the hard way."

"I see, so he regretted it, did he?"

"No. That was something he said he never did. He loved Hetty and he knew she loved him, and he was very positive about love, my dad.

"He was determined that there weren't to be any regrets about it for any reason—and this was true even before he knew that Hetty was expecting.

"When they found that out he was thrilled in spite of all the difficulties. He just saw it as a dilemma that had to be worked through in a loving way."

"Oh, and it was just my poor father's bad luck that he was caught in the middle of it."

"I suppose you could put it that way. Dad saw it as one of the dilemmas, one of the tragedies, that war brings."

And so, they talked on and on until John looked at his watch and gasped.

"Oh dear, is that the time? I teach at the Cathedral school, and if I don't run, I'll be late back."

"I'm sorry, it's my fault."

"Of course, it isn't. Now I meant it about coming to see us sometime and meeting my mum. She really would love that and so would I."

"Bye." He paid the bill and hurried off.

Liz realised when he'd gone that he'd paid for her too.

She got up slowly and walked back to the cemetery where she sat down again on the remembrance seat and thought for a long time, before catching the bus to the village and Mavis and Arnold.

---ooo000ooo---

Time passed very slowly and painfully for Will and Hetty. The four children got home as often as they could, as they had promised, but Will had to give up his job and for the most part he and Hetty were thrown entirely on each other's company.

As Will's cancer got worse, so his sarcasm increased in proportion—sarcasm that was directed almost entirely at Hetty.

All the children had now had the treatment that Will gave first of all to Liz and, with the exception of Mary, they were all horrified at their mother's treatment of their father during the war.

More than all Will's sarcasm, Hetty found this palpable resentment from her children hard to bear.

As usual Peggy was a source of encouragement, and she would catch the bus to see Hetty and Will once a week. It was difficult for the two women to talk on their own at all as Will's demands were constant, but at least he did not criticise Hetty while Peggy was there and she felt Peggy's unspoken sympathy.

Even though she had farther to come than Mary and the boys, Liz made sure that there weren't many weekends when she didn't come to see her father.

While her conversation with John in the churchyard at Wells had helped her to see the events of the war years in more perspective, so that she was able to be more normal with Hetty, she still found a great anger within herself at the way her father had been treated, both by the Japanese and by his own wife.

She tried to dismiss it as one of the tragedies of war, as John had called it, but found that she was still angry.

This also coloured her attitude to John. She had liked him and found herself thinking about him a lot—but her thoughts always ended with a flash of resentment that he had been so sympathetic towards her mother, Hetty.

Perhaps I should go and see Janet sometime, thought Liz, *as John suggested.*

But then she realised that John still lived at home with his mother, so that wouldn't do. She didn't want it to look as if she were doing exactly what he had suggested. He might read something into that!

It was Janet herself who got in touch in the end. She and Peggy had kept in touch by phone and when she heard how very poorly Will was, she decided to risk it and ask Hetty if she could come and stay with her for a while to help.

"I shall quite understand if it will make it too difficult.

"But perhaps if you could just say that I'm an old friend from Wells, he might accept my presence."

Hetty was at the end of her tether as Will had taken a turn for the worse and was bedridden and incontinent.

"Please do come. It would be such a help. Apart from anything else, it is so difficult even to get out to do the shopping."

And so, it was arranged.

Will, by this time, was too ill to take much notice of who was helping Hetty and seemed to accept Janet as the old friend she said she was.

His sarcasm ceased in her presence and Hetty began to pick up a bit of strength with another pair of hands to help with all the chores.

Liz was very surprised to find a stranger helping her mother when she got home the next weekend—and yet a stranger who seemed to be very much at home with her mother and who was obviously an old friend.

Hetty introduced her.

"I believe you met my son, John," she said to Liz

"Did you? You didn't tell me that." Hetty was surprised.

"Somehow there hasn't been an opportunity."

Liz didn't add that she hadn't mentioned it because she wasn't anxious to discuss the meeting with her mother or tell her how John had stood up for her.

"John very kindly bought me some lunch having found me wandering in the churchyard that weekend I went down to see Gran and Granddad.

"As Dad had told me about the baby you had in the war—Dorothy—I thought I'd have a look for her grave."

"Oh, and did you find it?"

"Yes, I found it.

"But Mum, how's Dad? Is it all right if I go straight in to see him now?"

"Yes, of course, but he's not too good today, I'm afraid, so be prepared."

"Will has told them all about Dorothy and David now, although in the past he has always forbidden me to do so," Hetty explained as Liz went upstairs.

"What's worst is that the cancer has brought all his anger and resentment to the fore, with the result that, with the exception of Mary, they are all very cross with me."

She wiped away a stray tear.

"I find it so difficult. The children love Will dearly and have never seen his more difficult side, so they are bound to resent me when he tells them.

"On the other hand, I don't feel I can tell them my side of the story. It sounds so lame anyway, when you look back at it, and I can understand why they think there's no excuse for what happened.

"I think they will probably turn and tear me apart when he dies."

"Poor you, Hetty. That's so unfair of Will. I don't care how ill he is.

"He knows how hard you and David tried to put things right."

"The real problem, I imagine, was his treatment in the Japanese Concentration Camp, and his anger over that was somehow transferred across to you."

"You'll just have to hang on."

"Hang on to all that you and David said to each other about not regretting what happened and enjoying the fruit of the love you had for one another…and I don't just mean Dorothy, I mean the way you both used your love for each other as a springboard to give love to others—you to Will and David to me."

"I don't know about that anymore. I just can't think straight about any of it at the moment."

"Well, believe me then. I know how hard you both tried. I think you were both wonderful "

"It's not surprising that you can't think about it at the moment—you must be exhausted emotionally and physically.

"Don't worry about it. Don't even think about it. Just hang on to hope and you'll find your way through somehow—you'll see."

---ooo000ooo---

The next weekend Liz stopped off at Wells on her way home, so that she could travel with Mavis and Arnold who were coming up to Harrow to see their son.

She always enjoyed talking to her grandmother and the feeling was mutual.

"Your mum wanted us to see him while he still recognises us. She told us not to be too shocked at his appearance.

"Poor Will, what a terrible way to die—and after all he went through in the war too. It all seems so unfair, doesn't it? And your poor mother must be absolutely exhausted. I know how demanding my son can be when he's in the mood!"

Liz suddenly remembered what John had said about Mavis and Arnold knowing all about her mother's wartime baby and apparently having come to terms with it. So she took her courage in both hands and thought she would ask them about it.

175

"Dad told me what happened during the war a little while ago."

"You mean what happened in the Concentration Camp?" Arnold pricked up his ears.

"As far as I know he's never told anyone about that, and he really should have you know, he really should have. It's not good to bottle it up."

Mavis agreed. "You need to talk about terrible experiences like that, I believe, to help you to come to terms with them."

"It wasn't the Concentration Camp he talked about. It was about Mum being unfaithful to him while he was away and having a baby."

"Oh." Mavis and Arnold were silent for a while.

That's blown it, thought Liz. *I shouldn't have mentioned it.*

Finally, Mavis spoke.

"Both Granddad and I were very angry about what happened at the time but you have to get it into perspective.

"Your dad had been assumed to be dead for over eighteen months and Mary had been very ill.

"Young people often acted impulsively during the war as though there was no tomorrow. Your parents married very quickly at the beginning of the war for this very reason."

"Thinking about it afterwards, when we were less angry, we began to realise that what went on between your mother and David was probably more in the realm of mutual comfort than anything else."

"And although they had planned to get married at the end of the war, they tried so hard to put everything right, you know, once they realised that your dad was alive and would be returning.

"If they had been selfish about it, they could have let your dad come home to a broken marriage."

"I see. But why did they never tell us about it? Why did Mum not tell us?"

"I don't know, but I expect she had her reasons."

"I don't suppose Will would have wanted her to," her granddad spoke up. "No man would."

"He sobbed and sobbed about it," Liz wiped away a tear herself.

"Poor you. I expect that in some way it's all become bound up with the misery of everything else that happened during the war and the sadness came because this is the first time he's been able to talk about it."

"I expect you're right," Liz left it at that.

"You mustn't think that your mum hasn't been a good wife to him," her Grandmother told her, "because she has, you know. She had to put up with a lot, particularly in the early years."

Liz could think of nothing else to say.

---ooo000ooo---

It was back at College towards the end of the next week, that Liz got a phone call from her mother on Friday morning.

"Liz love, I'm so sorry. Dad died last night." Liz could hear the tears in her voice.

"Oh Mum, Oh Mum, I can't believe it!

"I knew he was very bad last weekend, and I saw how upset Gran and Granddad were and that they didn't think they'd see him again, but somehow I didn't think it would be as soon as this."

"No, nor did I, or I would have asked everyone to come last weekend.

"Eddie and Matt weren't with us, were they, and Mary only popped over briefly.

"But on the other hand, he would have hated everyone standing round his bed and looking at him, and none of us would have wanted him to suffer a moment longer really.

"It was so dreadful for him."

"I know." Liz was glad that she was at least able to hold her voice steady even though she was crying.

"Are you all right, Mum? Do you want me to get on the next train? What's going to happen? What's got to be done?"

177

"There's nothing you can do at the moment. Janet is still here with me and she's been wonderful. I don't know how I would have managed without her.

"But I need you as well, of course, and Mary and the boys. Just come as soon as you can.

"I'm sure the College will understand if you tell them what's happened. The funeral is next Tuesday, so you should be able to get back to College next Wednesday or Thursday."

"How long is Janet staying with you? I'll get the fast train late this afternoon—so I should get home mid-evening."

"That will be lovely. Mary is coming over this afternoon and the boys should get here this evening as well. I think Janet will go home when you all arrive."

---ooo000ooo---

"Can I join you?"

Sitting on the train later that day, Liz was surprised by a question from the corridor.

It was John.

"What are you doing here? Yes, of course you can join me."

"Mum rang me and I thought you might be on this train and be glad of some company."

"I've been checking every carriage since I got on at Wells looking for you, but if you'd rather be on your own, just say. I shall quite understand."

"No, it's OK," Liz heard her polite voice. "That was kind of you."

She fell silent, not able to think of anything else to say, and wiped away a stray tear.

"I'm so sorry about your dad. Mum told me, of course. Somehow although you know it's coming, it's so hard to believe, isn't it?"

"Yes. I feel in a dream somehow and it seems as if I'm just going through the motions without knowing why."

"I needed to talk when Dad died. Somehow talking about him helped me to realise what had happened. But you may not be at that stage yet."

Liz let out a great gulp.

"My poor dad, my poor dad." She was suddenly aware that she could sob with John there and that he would understand. "It all seems so unfair."

John, put his arm round her shoulder.

"I know. Life's a pig sometimes and it always seems to be the nicest people that suffer most."

"Dad was always such fun. I don't know what I shall do without him. He was always there, somehow." And feeling John's comforting arm around her she turned her head and wept on his shoulder.

Another passenger looked in the carriage door and seeing the two young people engrossed in this way, shut the door and walked on.

John let her cry, holding her close and making comforting noises, but saying nothing.

Eventually she sat up and rummaged around for her handkerchief.

"Here you are, I brought a clean one with me."

"Thank you." She blew her nose hard.

"I'm sorry I've made you rather wet and I've ruined your clean hanky."

John laughed. "I've got another. You can keep that one."

"I've got some chocolate here. Would you like a piece?"

"Yes, please."

After that they sat comfortably talking about all that had happened and about his dad as well as hers, feeling like old friends, so that she hardly noticed that John had got her hand in his and was quietly stroking it.

"One of the things that helped me most, was something your mum used to say to my dad."

"Oh, what was that?"

"Well, apparently when your father first went missing, she was terribly upset, understandably and some people in the church helped her to realise that one way of coping with her

179

grief was to give the love she had for your father to other people.

"Let me see, what was the phrase they used to quote to each other—it was something like this, I think, '*What you forget in your grief is that you still need to give love as well as receive it.*' It's in several of their letters to each other."

"Have you seen their letters then?" Liz was astonished.

"Yes, and I'm sure Mum will show them to you sometime if you want to see them."

"They're quite amazing in some ways, particularly the one your mum wrote to my dad after Dorothy died."

"Oh, I'd like to see that sometime. What a mess it must have been for all of them."

It wasn't until they were nearly into London that she suddenly asked.

"But why are you on this train? You didn't catch it specially to find me, did you?"

"Half and half. I've been wanting to visit some old college friends for some time, and when Mum phoned and I realised you might be on this train, it suddenly became a must."

"Oh," Liz was suddenly polite and rather reserved again. "Thank you."

"Don't go all polite on me again," John gently teased. "Family, remember?"

"I told you we always regarded you lot as part of our family—so for me this was a natural thing to do for a…sister?!"

Liz laughed. "I think you've got the gift of the gab."

"How about a visit to Wells sometime after the funeral to make a break," John suggested just before they parted."

"There are lots of lovely walks on the Mendip Hills and I'd love to show them to you. You could stay with us too if you wanted. Mum would love to have you, I know."

"I don't know. Sometime perhaps, but I can't think of anything but Dad at the moment."

"No, of course not. But if you change your mind, just give us a ring. Here—take our telephone number."

---ooo000ooo---

The next few days had an air of relief as well as sorrow for the Thomas family. Hetty was absolutely exhausted and desolate but drew strength from her two daughters and two sons, and their joint sorrow gave a feeling of family unity that had left them in the last few months of Will's life.

His complaints about their mother's behaviour in the war had confused the boys and made them angry, in exactly the same way as Liz.

Mary, being older and with happy memories of the time in Wells, was also confused but found herself unable to be angry. David had been kind to her as a small child and her memories were all good.

Sitting round the meal table one day, Eddie suddenly asked, "Mother, what exactly did happen during the war and why were you unfaithful to Dad and what happened to the child you had?

"Dad was so upset about it—but thinking about it now, it seems out of character for you to have been like that. What really happened?"

Hetty took a deep breath. She had been dreading this question. As before, she didn't want to mar her children's memories of their father, but Janet had told her in no uncertain terms that she must be fair to herself as well.

"If you tell them the truth and try to explain what it felt like in the war when those awful telegrams came, I think they will come around in the end."

"The problem was that Will wouldn't let you tell them what had really happened. Try to explain why."

"David always said that the truth never hurt anyone in the long run; it was half-truths and lies and silence that damaged."

Liz held her breath as she saw the conflict in her mother's face.

"Just tell us the truth, Mum. We shall understand if you tell us the truth."

And so Hetty began.

She told them how she and Will had decided to bring forward their wedding at the outset of the war, like many other young people.

She told them of Mary's birth and their father's brief visit home to see her and then his final week with them both before he was sent abroad.

She told them of the dreadful day when she got the telegram telling her that Will was presumed dead and why she had gone down to Somerset eighteen months later at the invitation of their grandparents to get away from the bombing.

She told them about life in the village and how David had been kind to her asking her to help with the Youth Club and involving her at the school, together with the visit to see Henry V and their first walk together.

She told them about Mary's illness and near death. She told them of David's kindness in bringing presents from the school children for Mary.

Then it was time to tell them about the walk when Mary was just beginning to recover and how upset she had been and how David had comforted her—a comforting that had gone further than either of them had intended.

She paused there.

"I'm so sorry you all hate me so much for this." She couldn't hold back her tears.

"But you have to understand that it wasn't a premeditated event. I know it sounds feeble to say that it just happened. But it did!

"David and I did love each other, you see, and it didn't feel as if I was being unfaithful to your father, because I genuinely thought he was dead and that he wouldn't come back.

"You've all met Janet now, who David later married, well she had a telegram similar to mine, followed by another saying that her first husband's body had been found.

"That was what I expected. It wasn't that I had forgotten your father or stopped loving him or felt that I was being unfaithful to him. That didn't enter into it.

"Oh dear." She looked around at their faces.

"You're all grown up now. Even though I'm sure you can't understand the urgency with which people entered relationships during the war, as if there was no tomorrow, surely you can begin to understand what happened to David and me?"

By now the two girls were also crying and the boys quietly wiping away the odd tear.

It was Liz who was the first to answer.

"We've all been more or less in love by now, Mum, so we do understand what it must have been like for you."

"But I suppose we all feel that David must have taken advantage of you. Dad referred to him as 'that bastard', but by all accounts—I've met his son, John—he wasn't a bastard, but a nice person."

"His son would say that," was Eddie's quick comment.

Hetty smiled.

"Your dad always called him 'that bastard'. I think it was one of the ways he tried to come to terms with what had happened.

"But David's fault, if any, was that he was too kind. He loved me, you see, though we both knew that we could only be friends for the time being, no more."

"But on that day when I was so upset over Mary and David was trying to comfort me, I suddenly realised that I loved him and that's when it all got out of hand."

"I remember David," Mary spoke up suddenly.

"I've never talked about the time in Wells because I realised that you didn't want me to, but I do remember it, and I do remember how kind David was. I loved him too."

"Tell us about the baby, then," said Matt. "What happened to it?"

"David was wonderful when I told him I was expecting a baby, after just that one occasion, remember. He was delighted. Like a dog with two tails!"

"But of course, it was very difficult because I was living with your grandparents and they were horrified, as you can understand they would be.

183

"David found me somewhere else to live—with Janet in Wells—and that's where little Dorothy was born. Do you remember her, Mary?"

"I remember a baby and being a bit jealous about all the attention she was receiving, nothing much else."

"It was when she was about three months old that the second telegram came saying that your father was alive.

"Again, David was very good. Although we had planned to marry after the war, once we knew your father was alive, there was never any question but that I would go back to him."

"I still loved him too, you see."

"David said that he would give up his job as a teacher and look after Dorothy, taking in pupils for private tutoring to make ends meet. But then his mother intervened and moved into Wells and instead of giving up altogether, David just worked mornings while she looked after Dorothy."

"What happened to her?" This was Eddie's question.

"She died of measles with complications when she was four years old."

"And David? What happened to him?"

"He married Janet about six months after Dorothy died and he himself died about five years ago."

"He had two children, John and Madeleine. Liz has met John, I believe."

"Yes. I was so angry and upset and confused after Dad had told me about all this that I thought I would go to Wells and try to find the grave of the baby."

"Well I did, and at the same time I found David's grave too. And I was standing there shouting at it and stamping when John found me. He wasn't too pleased."

"Oh dear. I didn't know that. Poor John."

"He didn't mind too much when he realised who I was but I felt pretty mean, I can tell you. He was so nice."

"Oh yes. Like father like son, I suppose," Matt remarked.

"It wasn't like that. He was just kind."

"He also told me how Gran and Granddad came around and were actually at David's funeral, sitting next to Mum!"

184

"So next time I saw them I asked them about it and they told me that they'd come to realise over the years how hard David and Mum had tried to put everything right, and they'd become very fond of him."

And so, the story was told with tears all round but at last with some real understanding and the recriminations died down.

"Thanks for telling us, Mum," Eddie remarked finally.

"It must have been difficult for you to do that and although there are still a lot more questions I'd like to ask, at least I feel as if I begin to understand."

"Yes, thanks Mum." Liz gave her a hug and the others followed suit.

At least, thought Hetty, *they will feel able to talk to me about it now that it is out in the open and they know the truth.*

---ooo000ooo---

The funeral came and went with much sorrow and some relief that Will's suffering was now over.

In the end it was late afternoon on the Friday that Liz travelled back to college.

She had some course work she wanted to catch up on over the weekend and as the boys were still with Hetty, she thought *it would be a good thing to get back to Bath herself and come down again perhaps the following weekend.*

Her heart felt heavy as she sat on the train, miserable at the thought of her lonely room in Bath as most of her friends would be away for the weekend. She should have stayed longer in Harrow.

She could have taken John up on his offer of a break in Wells this weekend, of course. She smiled at the thought and wished she had. She hadn't felt like it when he mentioned it before the funeral, but now she realised that she would like to talk and John was a good listener.

She was also curious to see the letters between David and Hetty that John had mentioned now that her mother had told them the story of what had happened during the war.

Oh well, I should have thought about it earlier, she thought, *it's too late now.* But she couldn't resist looking out of the window when the train drew into Wells and to her surprise there was John running up and down the platform.

What on earth is he doing? He must be meeting someone, I suppose, and irrationally she felt terribly disappointed that he wasn't meeting her. She sat back down.

"Hurry along there, please," shouted the guard. "Hurry up, sir, you must get on now or stand away from the train."

What was he doing? Liz stood up again. And there was John at the window. He opened the door.

"What on earth?"

"I just hoped you might be on this train and that I might be able to persuade you to change your mind and stop off here after all." John was panting a little after all his running.

"I've got work to do in Bath, that's why I'm going back today."

"Oh," John's face looked so crestfallen. "Are you sure it can't wait till Sunday. Couldn't you just stop one night?"

"Well…"

The guard was getting impatient.

"Hurry along please. Close the doors now please."

"Quick, hand me down your bag. Come on. One night won't make much difference. You need a break."

"Stand away now please…"

And before she knew what had happened, Liz was standing on the platform beside John and the train was pulling away from the platform. In one way she felt quite cross.

"Now look what you've done. And I'd planned to get so much work done too."

"I'm terribly sorry, I'll come and help you with your work—that's a promise." John looked and felt very guilty.

"I was coming past the station and heard the train coming and suddenly thought you might be on it."

"I'm so sorry. How thoughtless of me! I really will come and help you with your work if you like."

Suddenly Liz laughed.

"You're good at Home Economics, are you then? That's my main subject."

And having started to laugh she couldn't stop and John joined in too until they were both helpless and holding on to each other.

"What would you have done if I hadn't been on the train?" asked Liz finally.

"Heaven alone knows. I was so worried about you that I might even have got on the train and tried to look you up in Bath…"

"But as I don't know either your address or telephone number, that would have been very complicated. But obviously in my present mood I could have done anything!"

"What on earth were you worried about me for?" Liz was puzzled. "You knew I'd be sad, I suppose, but that's normal."

"Well," John looked slightly embarrassed.

"I suppose it must mean that I care about you and don't like the thought of you feeling sad."

Now it was Liz's turn to feel embarrassed and felt herself blushing.

"Come on." John noticed her embarrassment. "Let's go and find a cup of tea somewhere. That's the first priority, so that I can catch up a bit on your news."

He picked up her bag and they set off down the road, chatting easily.

"Mum told us about David and Dorothy last week," she told him over tea.

"It cleared the air and helped a lot. I think we all understand a bit better now, though I was thinking on the train that I would like to see those letters you mentioned if you wouldn't mind."

"That must be it. Thought transference!"

"What on earth are you talking about now?"

"Well, I must have picked up your vibes when you were thinking on the train and that's why I suddenly found myself running up and down the platform looking for you."

Liz burst out laughing.

"That's right! Blame me now for your foolishness. Words fail me!"

John laughed too and once again their laughter almost threatened to get out of hand.

"I think we'd better get out of here before they ask us to go." John noticed that the chatter in the rest of the café had died down and people were looking at them.

"Let's go home and find Mother and tell her that you're staying the night."

"Are you sure that will be all right?"

"Of course," said John. "She'll be as pleased as punch, you'll see."

"Later on, if you're not too tired and haven't yet seen it, *West Side Story* is on at the cinema."

"No, I haven't seen it and I've been wanting to. That would be lovely."

As predicted, Janet was delighted to see Liz and welcomed her warmly.

"Do tell me how the funeral went and above all how your mum is. She was so exhausted after all those weeks when your dad was so very poorly."

"I think she's OK. But we were all feeling so punch drunk that I suppose it is early days yet."

"Incidentally, Mum told us how wonderful you were to her during the war and about all that happened with David and Dorothy. You were so kind to them."

"And she was so grateful for all your help with Dad these last few weeks too. She said that it made all the difference."

"It helped us all too, to have met you and found out what a nice person you were for ourselves when she was telling us about David."

"Good. Somehow it all seemed very natural as David and I always regarded Hetty as part of the family, and as a result Will and the rest of you were just part of our extended family too."

"That's what John said." Liz suddenly wondered if John still regarded her as just a sister and felt a little disappointed at the prospect.

"Liz said that she would like to see the letters between David and Hetty sometime, Mum," said John.

"Yes, of course." Janet went to fetch them.

It was Hetty's letter to David after Dorothy's death that Janet found first for Liz, who read it in silence and then sat looking rather glum.

"I know why you're silent," said Janet. "She talks about your dad being difficult and that is hard for you.

"But you have to realise as Hetty and David did, that it wasn't his fault he was difficult; it was the result of the treatment he had received during the war."

"I think time will tell that those poor prisoners not only received terrible physical treatment and beatings like your father, but also grave psychological damage, which doesn't heal easily, and it wasn't just your dad who suffered in this way."

"I see. Nothing was ever said about anything like this to us, so you can understand why it was so difficult for us to understand. And Dad was a wonderful father.

"We only very occasionally saw the other side of him and the way he could be horrible to Mum, when we came upon them unexpectedly. He was also very sarcastic to her in front of us sometimes."

"I know. Your mother must have loved him very much to be able to cope with it the way she did."

"I'm sorry to interrupt, but if we're going to get to *West Side Story*, we ought to be leaving in a minute." John was getting his coat on. "It starts at seven o'clock but I expect we'll have to queue for at least half an hour if we want to get in."

"Oh dear, and you haven't had anything to eat," Janet was dismayed.

"We had tea and cakes in Café Royale and we can get some Fish and Chips when it's over, so don't worry about it, Mum."

"I'll leave out the other two main letters for you to look at when you get in. I may get an early night as I've got a good book!"

189

I wish this wasn't a tragedy, thought Liz, *remembering the Romeo and Juliet theme of the film, as the excitement of the music and dance and the danger of the blossoming screen romance swept over her.*

John glanced at her enwrapped face and felt for her hand which stayed in his for the rest of the performance.

There was hardly a dry eye as they left the cinema and Liz's small handkerchief had long since been soaked through and stuffed back in her pocket, while she went on to use a clean one that John produced—though even he, like most of the men, had been forced to blow his nose more than once.

People crept quickly away from the bright lights of the cinema ashamed for others to see how much they had been affected by what was, after all, only a film.

"It's the waste of it all that makes me so angry," Liz was indignant. "The terrible waste! Why waste a wonderful love like that, that crossed boundaries. It could have brought them all together if only they'd let it. It all seems so futile!"

"I know. It seems so terrible, doesn't it, that other people should try to dictate whom you should love and how."

"It's so stupid, too, because love makes a mockery of the boxes, we try to squeeze it into and bursts out where it's least wanted and least convenient.

"That poor girl. How could she live on with a tragedy like that on her mind? She must have blamed herself too, although of course it wasn't her fault. I don't think I could go on living in those circumstances."

"And yet, if Maria had killed herself in true Juliet style, she would have lost all that Tony was trying to achieve."

"At least by living on and being recognised by his friends as having been his girl, she was trying to carry on the reconciliation he had been working for. And that's what he would have wanted, of course."

Their discussions and arguments continued as they bought their fish and chips and walked home.

Janet had gone to bed when they got in but had left out some of David and Hetty's letters to each other, as promised. John picked them up.

"Here are the first two. As you can see from this first letter my Dad wrote to Hetty, he was hopelessly in love with her, but he wasn't careless about your Dad either.

"He just thought he most probably wouldn't come back from the war, and that it was a pity not to express his love in some way—even if it wasn't physical.

"Look, there's the bit I quoted to you the other day, *'What you forget in your grief is that you still need to give love as well as receive it.'* They were always quoting that at each other!"

He passed it to Liz, who read on.

Will you allow me at least to declare my love to you and to try to make you happy—even though we know that we may never be able to marry?

"Must time, or lack of it, limit loving? Don't you think, perhaps, that love is God-given in all its forms and that it should never be kept selfishly to oneself but always shared in some way?'

Already emotionally overstretched by the film on top of the recent death of her father, Liz suddenly found her tears flowing again.

John pulled her gently to her feet and put his arms round her, holding her tight.

"I'm sorry," he said softly into her hair. "I'm so sorry. I should have realised. It's the wrong time to show them to you just after the death of your father. What a fool I am, I should have realised."

"It's not that," Liz tried hard to control herself.

"It's just that it's all so sad and impossible. Is love, real love, always as sad as the film and as that letter?"

"I think they were just unlucky," John wiped her tears away gently and thoughtfully.

191

"There is always a risk, of course, but if you never risked anything you would never do anything worth doing, would you?"

"What do you think?" He held her eyes with his, anxious to know if she minded his touch, as he realised he wanted to kiss her very badly.

"I suppose I believe in risk taking too, within limits of course!"

"Of course." Then he kissed her on her lips very gently and with the spectre of his father and her mother in his mind.

"Do you like that sort of risk?"

For reply she returned his kiss, before pulling back and saying, "But I think that women always have to risk much more than men and that doesn't seem fair to me."

"You're right, of course," John kissed her again, still gently.

She felt herself warm to the tenderness in his lips, a tenderness she had never experienced before.

"But if the woman trusts the man and he is trustworthy, then surely there isn't the same risk. Your mum was right to trust my dad because his response to what happened simply illustrated the sort of person he was, didn't it?"

"I suppose so. I suppose some men would have just walked away and left her. Mum's not stupid. She must have trusted David to allow what happened, to happen."

Both their thoughts were busy for a moment, with Liz especially reviewing all that had happened to her mother in her mind, while John realised that he had to wait for her to make the next move.

She broke the silence.

"As you say, he must have been a good man." She reached up and kissed him softly again and again realised how good it felt.

But then she remembered.

"My brothers still thought it must have been his fault when Mum told them about it."

"And what do you think?" John hardly dared to wonder what her answer would be.

Liz pulled away for a moment and was silent, looking up at him seriously, while he returned her look equally seriously and gently stroked her hand.

"I think it takes two to kiss," she said finally, half laughing.

John let out a shout of laughter and then picked her up and started dancing round the room with her, singing.

"Mar... Eliza, I've just met a girl called Eliza. And suddenly I've found... I'll never be the same again."

Liz was laughing too.

"For goodness sake don't make such a noise. You'll wake your mother."

"She doesn't mind my singing. Do you?"

He spun her round again but then tripped over the leg of a chair and they both landed in a heap on the settee, their laughter gradually dying out as their lips met, half laughing to begin with, but then more seriously and urgently.

"You'd be more comfortable on my lap."

"I think you're just trying to get me into a compromising position." Liz was half laughing, telling herself to draw away, but nevertheless reluctant to do so.

"Just one comfortable kiss and then I'll let you go, I promise. You don't really think I'd compromise you, do you?"

He looked rather anxious again, but her lips were on his before he could worry and their comfortable kiss went on for a very long time before Liz got slowly to her feet and made her way towards the door.

"How about a walk tomorrow before I put you on the train back to Bath?"

"That would be lovely. I'd better get some beauty sleep in first then."

"Goodnight, see you in the morning."

"Goodnight... Eliza..." His words caressed her as she climbed the stairs.

---ooo000ooo---

The next day dawned fine and warm. Janet packed them a picnic and they decided to make their way to Wookey Caves and back and also promised her to see if they could find some blackberries as she wanted to make a blackberry and apple pie.

She laughed as she gave them the picnic.

"Be careful, that was the fateful walk your dad and Hetty took."

"That was then, this is now," said John firmly.

"Thanks for leaving those other letters out for me last night. It all helps to fit the puzzle together, doesn't it?" Liz got her coat on.

To begin with they walked separately, silently and fast, each engrossed with their own thoughts while nevertheless enjoying the late summer sun and stopping every now and then as they saw blackberries almost falling to the ground, they were so ripe.

It's almost as if we're afraid to touch each other today, thought Liz, *wondering if last night's kissing had just been a flash in the pan, as these things sometimes were.* Once again, she wondered if John did really think of her as a sister and nothing more! Oh dear, she couldn't believe that—not after last night!

She had been kissed before and she had been, or had fancied herself, in love before. But kissing John last night had been quite different. His kisses had been so tender and made her feel he really cared about her. Never had kissing seemed so normal and natural before, either, or such fun.

She smiled as she remembered the way he had danced around with her in his arms.

I'm in a bad way, I've fallen in love with him, she thought.

Now she found she positively hurt as she looked at John's back, as he strode ahead of her, and she longed for him to turn around and take her hand.

At the same moment her grief over her father's death flooded back too, especially as she realised that she had fallen in love with someone he would definitely not have approved of.

As if on cue, John turned and reached out his arm to her, taking her hand.

"Penny for them. What are you thinking about so seriously that it's making you sad again?"

"How do you know?"

"It must be that thought transference again." John laughed, but then seeing her face, he became serious.

"Liz, it was wonderful being with you last night. I badly want to go on seeing you, you know, and I badly want to go on kissing you too."

"I enjoyed it too," Liz sounded rather flat, "and you made me forget how sad I am for a short time."

John put his arms around her.

"I'm sorry it's so hard for you at the moment. I remember how terrible it is when the grief comes flooding back in and you feel guilty because you've forgotten it for a moment."

He understands, thought Liz. *Thank goodness, he understands.*

"Tell me about your father. I wish I'd had the chance to meet him."

Hand in hand they walked on and as they walked, Liz talked about her father and how he had always made her feel so special because he was so proud of her.

"He had no reason to be. He was just that kind of father."

"I don't blame him. Anybody would be proud of you."

"That's why it was so awful when he broke down after he'd been to see me play Ophelia in Hamlet and told me about what happened in the war. It was such a shock."

"It must have been terrible for you, and for your mother too, I suppose."

John pulled her gently to him and kissed her forehead and they stood quietly together for a minute, each enjoying the nearness of the other, before walking on again in companionable silence, each thinking their own thoughts.

I want to tell her I love her, thought John, who had been trying to sit on his feelings all morning, realising that for the moment, Liz's grief had got the upper hand and he must help her with it.

After they had found Wookey Hole, though, and eaten so many blackberries that their hands were sticky, their mood changed.

"Hetty and Dad didn't get as far as here. Come on, let's explore."

"Are you sure it's safe?" Liz was a little apprehensive.

"I'll carry you if it will make you feel safer."

"Safer!" Liz laughed.

"I remember what happened last night! I'm not stupid!"

John laughed too and they explored hand in hand instead, marvelling at the stalactites and stalagmites which were plainly visible even just in the limited light from the doorway.

Liz shivered as they reached the entrance again.

"Are you cold?"

John pulled her to him to warm her and kissed her at the same time, a kiss that she returned with equal tenderness.

"Why is it so nice when we kiss?" she asked as they stood encircled in each other's arms.

"I think it's probably because we love each other. Or at least, I love you."

Liz was embarrassed but felt her heart flutter at the same time and a great joy fill her that she couldn't yet identify or acknowledge.

"I was trying to think of a way of saying it without frightening you off—and now I've done it, and you probably will be frightened off! But never mind, we talked about risk last night and I've now taken the risk of telling you that I love you. I'm sorry. I hope you don't mind."

"I've come to the conclusion that I like people who take risks."

"Meaning?"

"That I like you."

"Is that all?" his voice was still very quiet as if he hardly dared to hear the answer.

"Is that all?"

"No. I love you too. At least if I don't, I don't know what all this hurting is about."

"What hurting?" John was puzzled.

"When we started off this morning and you were striding ahead, I suddenly thought that perhaps you just thought of me as a sister, and that hurt."

"Then you've been so kind, letting me talk about my dad, and we've been so friendly together that I thought perhaps that was what we were. Just good friends."

"Good heavens! A sister! Just a friend! Whatever next! Of course, I don't think of you as a sister or as just a friend!

"I don't kiss my sister or my friends—or at least not in the way I kiss you. Nor do I want to kiss them all the time, as I want to kiss you."

"Well, sometimes people kiss just for fun."

"I don't know who else has been kissing you, but I thought that last night was different, didn't you?

"I love you, Liz, and when I kiss you, I want to tell you I love you.

"Come here, perhaps I need to give you a few more lessons in what it is all about."

Liz laughed and allowed herself to be kissed but the tenderness of it took her breath away, so that she drew back again quite quickly.

"Remember your mother's warning. We've got to get to Wookey and back and pick some blackberries for her."

John laughed too.

"We're safe now. We've been to Wookey and we're on our way back."

They walked on laughing, swinging their hands.

"Liz, when I told you that I love you, I didn't mean it to stop there, you know."

"What do you mean?"

"I mean that though it's far too soon after your father's death to ask you, I don't want you to think that I just love you today and that I will forget about it tomorrow when you go back to college…

"I love you so much that I want to marry you. That's the way I love you."

"Oh."

Liz was lost for words again and John noticed the colour come and go in her face.

"I'm such a blundering fool. It's far too soon to tell you all this."

"But I can't bear the thought of you going back to college tonight and waking up tomorrow morning thinking this is all a dream. You won't do that, will you?"

"It doesn't sound as if you're going to let me do that, though I find it hard to believe you really mean it. You're not just being kind to me again?"

Liz was so overwhelmed that she felt quite shy.

"Liz, of course I'm not just being kind to you. What on earth can I do to make you believe me?"

"I love you!" he shouted suddenly at the top of his voice, making some nearby walkers stop and stare.

"Shush!"

Liz was laughing now, and John joined in.

"I believe you; I believe you. I'll do anything you say. And what's more, you're impossible and I love you!"

"Well, at least that's a beginning."

They were still laughing as they leant nearer and nearer till their lips were touching once again.

"But will you take the risk of my brothers regarding you as 'that bastard's' son. There's a lot of their father in them, you know."

Liz was suddenly fearful again and John was swift to reassure her, holding her close.

"As long as you love me and you can cope with it, I can cope with it too, never fear. And anyway, they'll come around in time."

Gradually as they walked on, joy filled them, and they had to keep stopping to see once again the expression in each other's eyes and to reassure each other with yet another kiss.

Their walk was taking far longer than intended.

It was John who noticed the time first.

"Liz, I'm terribly sorry, but I think you've just missed your train on to Bath!"

"Oh dear! I completely forgot the time."

"You'll just have to stay another night."

John couldn't keep the delight out of his voice or his eyes.

"You're hopeless. You might at least look a bit remorseful about making me miss my train."

Liz couldn't keep the happiness out of her eyes but tried at least to make her voice sound so prim that John laughed out loud again.

"Liz, I do love you so much!"

They laughed together again.

"Hey, we must tell our mums—I wonder what on earth they will think! I suppose, I really ought to ask your mum if I can have your hand in marriage. Do you think she'll say yes?"

Liz laughed

"She'll be thrilled, I'm sure. How about yours?"

"She'll be over the moon. Perhaps it would be nice to tell them together sometime. What do you think? Or should we spring it on Mum when we get home now?"

"It would be nicer to wait a bit and tell them together if we can."

---ooo000ooo---

Janet was looking quite worried when they eventually got home.

"Well Liz would dawdle so; I just couldn't hurry her up at all."

"I like that. He just wouldn't stop talking so I had to keep standing still and listening to him."

They both laughed and Janet joined in. Looking from one shining face to the other she soon had a very good idea of what had really happened, and she was pleased.

"I take it you're going to stay an extra night. That's wonderful news. I had so hoped you would be able to stay a little longer.

"In fact, I was already planning on a good meal just in case, to get your strength up again after all your energetic walking, as I'm sure you don't eat properly at college."

"I've got some news for you too. Your mum's just been on the phone and she is coming down here to stay for a few days later in the week. So why not visit next weekend as well, while she's here?"

"Oh, please do, Liz. That would be wonderful."

"Well, I suppose if I work till midnight every day this week, I could just about manage the time…"

"Great!"

Later on, when they were on their own for a minute they made plans.

"We can tell them both next week when your mum's here. Oh Liz, it's only just beginning to dawn on me that you've said you love me and you'll marry me and I'm so excited."

"Me too. I have this sort of warm pleased feeling inside that won't go away."

John laughed and gave her a hug.

---ooo000ooo---

Hetty was glad to get away from Harrow the following Wednesday afternoon. It was good of Janet to ask her to stay and a break away from all the memories of Will's illness and those awful last few months would be a great help.

She would spend most of Thursday with Mavis and Arnold, she thought, *and then she would be free to spend the rest of the time with Janet.*

Somehow, death put everything in perspective and she badly needed time to unpack her feelings about Will and to some extent her feelings about her time with David all those years ago. Janet would be a good listener, she knew.

She might also help her with the furious anger she was now feeling both against Will and to a lesser extent against David, which was all interspersed and muddled up with her grief.

Her life had been such a mess. None of it had gone to plan. She had lost David a long time ago and now she had lost Will.

What was left for her now? Who was she now? Both David and Will had died young and here she was in her late fifties and life was closing in around her.

On top of everything else, she was exhausted. She felt as if she'd spent her whole life running, trying to keep Will happy, trying to keep the house running smoothly, trying to help the children to find their way in life.

Then as soon as the children had left home—and Liz was the last just over two years ago—Will had been taken ill.

There had never been any time to do any of the things she wanted. Never even been the time to find out who she was and what she herself wanted to do.

Her whole life seemed to have been spent reacting to one emergency after another or trying to cope with one problem after another.

Hetty sighed as she stared out of the window, seeing but not seeing the countryside as it flashed by.

"Wells, Wells," the porter's voice jolted her out of her reverie and she sprang to her feet, reaching up to the rack for her case.

Suddenly the door opened and a voice said, "Can I help you with that, Mrs Thomas?"

It was John. Hetty hadn't seen him since David's funeral, but it wasn't difficult to recognise him. He was so like his father.

"That's very kind of you. I was half asleep and didn't realise where we had got to until the porter shouted out Wells."

"I wasn't expecting anyone to meet me because your mum said that she didn't finish work until five o'clock and it's only 4.45."

"Being a teacher, I finish earlier. Or at least I finish at school earlier, and then, of course, have to spend the evening marking and preparing."

"Do you enjoy teaching? I know your father did and he was very good at it too. He was very popular with his pupils."

"Yes, I love it. Or at least most of the time I do. I had to try to cope with some bullying today, which wasn't much fun."

---ooo000ooo---

Thursday spent with Mavis and Arnold was not an easy day. Their sadness was made worse, like Hetty's, by anger.

And they were angry not only about Will's illness and death but also about the treatment he received in the Concentration Camp during the war, which they rightly saw as the root of many of his subsequent problems.

The trouble was that their memories of the war revived their memories of the time Hetty spent with them and of the subsequent birth of Dorothy and all the problems that entailed.

Hetty was glad that she hadn't arranged to stay long and got on the bus for Wells with a sigh of relief.

Tomorrow she would have time to herself, she thought. *Tomorrow she could do exactly what she wanted for once.*

But when tomorrow came, she found that there was not a lot that she really wanted to do and having visited the Cathedral and walked round the shops twice, making her feet ache, she decided to go and look at the graveyard where David and Dorothy were buried.

She sat in the teak seat that overlooked them and gradually the jumble of her thoughts cleared and she remembered so well their time together, going through all their conversations in her mind once again and once again wishing and wishing that there could have been a different outcome.

Oh, she had been happy enough with Will in spite of the bad times and the children were wonderful. She wouldn't be without them.

But she knew that happiness with David would have been of a different order. She remembered how he tried to set up reminders of their love, with the trees they both bought and planted in their gardens, to support her. She remembered his wonderful letters. She remembered their song and her tears started to flow again.

She sat there a long time and had just realised that she had better move as she was getting cold, when she heard laughter in the distance. Funny, she could have sworn that was Liz's laugh, but it couldn't be. She had telephoned Liz and told her not to come home as she was coming away this weekend. Unless…

The laughter came nearer and then around the corner came Liz and John, holding hands and laughing.

They stopped when they saw her. Hetty hurriedly tidied away her tears and hoped they hadn't noticed.

"The very person we were looking for! I've just picked Liz up from the train from Bath and we were taking a short cut home through the cemetery hoping to find you here and surprise you. You didn't know she was coming to stay too, did you!"

"No, I certainly didn't! Liz, how lovely to see you. What a surprise! Why didn't you tell me that you were going to be here too? Poor Janet with two visitors!"

"Well, I'm afraid I deliberately didn't tell you," said Liz.

"Why on earth not?" Hetty was mystified.

"As John said, we wanted to surprise you."

"And the more visitors we have, the happier Mum is."

Hetty looked from one face to another and seeing the happiness in their eyes began to understand.

"Have I time to treat you both to a cup of tea at the Café Royale before your mum gets home from work?"

"That would be lovely. We were there last weekend."

"Last weekend! I thought you went straight back to college to catch up with your work, Liz. What made you change your mind?"

"John dragged me off the train."

They both burst out laughing and John explained that he was just passing the station when he heard the train and so on.

"It all sounds rather feeble trying to explain it to you."

"But although I was a bit cross to begin with, I'd been feeling miserable on the train and I was really glad. It helped to get a break before getting down to work again. I had to work very hard this week to catch up though."

Hetty joined in their laughter as they made their way to the teashop and realised as she did so that it was the first time she had really laughed for a very long time.

"That poor porter. He was at his wits' end with me."

"I wish I could have seen you running up and down the platform looking for her."

Their laughter began again and Hetty felt the first stirring of happiness as she sat and listened to them chatting and laughing but nevertheless careful to include her in the conversation too.

As they left the teashop to walk the short distance home, John caught hold of Hetty's arm.

"Mrs Thomas. Will you do me the honour of letting me have your daughter's hand in marriage?"

Hetty gasped, went red and then white and then started to laugh and cry all at once.

"I'd no idea. I'd no idea. You certainly seem very happy together. How wonderful!"

"Yes, of course I'll let you marry Liz. Provided she agrees, of course. This is fantastic news. You've no idea! It's just fantastic!"

Liz leant across John.

"That's what happened last weekend, Mum. We found out that we loved each other."

"But you haven't known each other very long. Are you sure?"

"I know it's rather soon to talk about marriage, but I couldn't bear the idea of Liz sitting all lonely at college and wondering whether the love we had discovered was just a flash in the pan or not. I wanted her to know I was really serious about it. That's why I asked her to marry me."

How like David, thought Hetty. *He used to worry about things like that.*

"Of course, we know we can't do anything about it yet, until I've finished college, but it makes all the difference somehow to know that we belong together."

"And your mum, what does she think?"

"We haven't told her yet. We wanted to tell you together if possible, but then I realised that I had to ask your permission first. We'll tell Mother as soon as we all get home."

"And what would you have done if I'd refused my permission?"

John and Liz looked at each other and burst out laughing once again.

"I'm afraid, Mum, that we would probably eventually have gone ahead and got married anyway—after trying very, very hard to persuade you first, of course."

Hetty laughed too.

"I hoped you'd say that. But thank you for asking me all the same."

Janet was as delighted as Hetty when they got home and told her.

"I had guessed something was afoot. You should have seen their faces when they got home from their walk last Saturday. They positively glowed!"

"Let's see if *The Crown and Anchor* can fit us all in for a celebratory meal this evening. We can't let this pass without some sort of festivity."

"What about a ring? Have you got a ring yet?"

"I thought we could shop for that together tomorrow—unless Liz has other ideas on the subject, of course. I've seen one or two lovely ones that I want to show her."

"How exciting!"

Liz was delighted.

It was only towards the end of their meal together that the conversation became more serious.

"I hope you don't mind, Mum, but when John saw how upset I was about all that Dad had said about David and what happened in the war, he asked Janet if I could see some of the letters you and David wrote to each other."

"Yes, I didn't think you would mind, Hetty, as you knew I'd seen them. I was going to give them back to you this weekend, actually, as I thought that you should keep them now.

"We've just been keeping them for you. But I thought you'd be happy for your children to see them in the same way that David showed them to our children."

"You made so many sacrifices and they've come to mean a great deal to all of us."

"They're wonderful letters, Mum. You were so brave about it all and I'm so proud of you."

"Oh," Hetty was rather doubtful.

"I know how difficult it must be even to think about it at the moment."

"Everything always seems so confused after a death and you think you'll never be able to fit the jigsaw together again."

"That's right. I'm finding it very hard to think straight at all at the moment."

Then Liz butted in, "They all knew what happened right from the beginning because as you know both David and Janet loved you and so they told their children about it all and it became as if you were part of the family—and us by extension!"

"I see." Hetty smiled at Liz's eagerness in spite of herself. "I see."

"Mum has always said that she is particularly grateful to you for writing that letter to Dad after Dorothy died and so am I."

"Don't you remember, I told you that too? I'm sorry, Hetty. I hope this isn't too painful for you at the moment. These young people are so eager, there's no stopping them."

"No, no, it's all right. It's better said. But…but I still don't see how all these things affect the next generation, affect John?"

Liz leant over and took her mother's hand.

"Mum, don't you see…" she started.

"Don't you see," John butted in and continued, "if you hadn't written that and helped Dad to see that he couldn't just go on hugging his grief to himself, he might never have got together with Mum and I wouldn't have been born!"

"And if you hadn't gone back to Dad, I would never have been born either!"

"I begin to see your reasoning." Hetty began to laugh.

"That phrase you used to use to each other, what was it now… I know, '*What you forget in your grief is that you need to give love as well as receive it.*' That's what helped Dad."

"You see, it's all your fault that we met and fell in love and are going to get married!"

Perhaps something good really was coming out of all that unhappiness, thought Hetty.

Perhaps her life had not been such a complete mess after all. Perhaps she would eventually be able to look back and make sense of it all.

It was not just ordinary good news about John and Liz. It was wonderful news.

---ooo000ooo---

Next morning when John and Liz left to shop for their engagement ring, Hetty and Janet made for the Post Office.

Hetty picked up a telegram form and addressed it to Peggy.

It read:

Wonderful news. David's son, John, and Liz are to be married. Who said there were never any happy endings!

The End